Gulf Dreams
A Chase Gordon Tropical Thriller
Douglas Pratt

MANTA PRESS

Gulf Dreams is a work of fiction. Any names, places, characters, and incidents are products of the author's imagination or are used fictitiously. Any resemblance to actual persons, either living or dead, events, or locales is entirely coincidental.

Copyright © 2023 by Douglas Pratt

Cover art by

Ryan Schwarz

The Cover Designer

www.thecoverdesigner.com

All rights reserved.

For Ashlee

1

The clouds overhead were light and fluffy, an off-white mix of cotton and cotton candy. They drifted from one side of the sky to the other at an unhurried pace. As they seemed to sway from side to side with an almost supernatural grace, their shade of white was a perfect complement to the deep blue ocean. I could faintly make out a few wispy tendrils that looked like smoke from a chimney.

I felt the heat vanish as the thick veil shielded me from the rays of the Florida sun. I couldn't see anything but the sky. I was lying on the foredeck of *Carina*, dozing slightly after finishing the last of the blue crab salad I made the night before. The mixture filled two pieces of toasted bread perfectly, and I washed it down with a cold bottle of Pacifico. It was a well-deserved meal. The nap after even more so. I'd spent the morning in the water. Not doing anything fun, like spearfishing or snorkeling. No, I was scraping barnacles off the hull of my forty-foot Tartan sailboat.

The work was tedious, and I'd let the task go undone for too long. Luckily, I donned my scuba gear, making the undertaking easier than continuously diving below in a snorkel. After an hour and a half of chopping away at the little bastards with a putty knife, I surfaced, feeling I could now avoid this chore for a couple of months.

That seemed like a perfectly good reason to lounge this afternoon. Besides, I had nothing on the agenda now.

The ocean air was salty, with a faint hint of fish. The waves lapped against the hull of the boat, creating a gentle, hypnotizing melody. At the moment, I couldn't think of a better place to be.

Carina, my floating home, bobbed at anchor in nine feet of water just off of Rabbit Key, an island about twelve miles from Islamorada in the Florida Keys. I lowered the hook to the sandy bottom about four days ago. So far, the only signs of life I'd seen were three different fishing boats puttering around the mangroves in the early morning. Well, I guess when I said life, I meant people. A small pod of dolphins dropped by every evening to swim around the boat.

I wasn't sure I'd spoken a word in the last two days, partly because I spent a good portion of those days breathing through a mouthpiece attached to my regulator, hacking away at barnacles on the hull of *Carina*. The trouble with barnacles was that no matter how hard you scraped a diver's pick at them, they still clung tighter than a crab clutching its shell. At some point I considered that an angle grinder would be faster. While cleaning the hull, I could only utter frustrated groans and bear it until it was clean.

Besides, who was I going to talk to?

That wasn't a complaint on my part, though. I loved solitude. And if I could find that on the ocean, that was even better. Even those menial boat jobs like hull scraping seemed to be better out here.

I rolled over onto my stomach and reached for the well-worn paperback I picked up from the book pile at the marina in Marathon. Its cover depicted a rugged character with a gun, standing on a rooftop in some European capital. I'd been reading it for a week now, following a burned ex-CIA assassin as he fought an intense battle across Europe. It felt thrilling and far-fetched, but then I supposed most fiction did.

As I flipped open to the folded page, the cloud moved along, letting the ultraviolet rays beam down on my bare back. Since getting out of the Marine Corps, I'd spent most of my days on board *Carina*. If I wasn't working up in West Palm Beach to fill up my bank account, then I was at sea. My bronzed skin was the result. I bought sunscreen by the case and kept it applied because despite my skin's built-up tolerance to burning, I preferred to stave off any chances of skin cancer.

It rained a lot in the Keys, but the rainfall never lasted more than a day. When it rained, the clouds rolled in from the Gulf like a slow-moving tsunami in the sky. The dark clouds were always welcome because they promised relief from the sweltering heat. The rain hit like warm, wet bullets, creating an excellent opportunity to collect fresh water. Since my four solar panels mounted on an arch over the stern of *Carina* powered everything but the air conditioner, I didn't need to make my way to civilization anytime soon if I replenished my tanks.

A cool, consistent breeze rolled between the islands from the Gulf. The gentle wind replaced the humid heat with a soft caress.In fact, a lot of newcomers to the area fell prey to the sun's rays, mistaking the cool wind for milder weather than it actually was. I'd see them in the hotel lobbies and bars, their skin bright red and tight from their carelessness.

I peered up at the clouds that seemed to gather like kids plotting some mischief. Eventually, they'd merge, bursting out in a quick shower. If it even got to me, the rain wouldn't last five minutes—ten at the most. It might be enough to wash off the salt water and maybe shampoo my hair.

The words on the page didn't excite me, and I let my head lower on the towel protecting me from the hot fiberglass deck. My eyes closed. The only thing I heard was the soft slap of waves against the hull. Today morphed from a shitty job into a pretty nice day. It was that way with life at sea. I called it the suck-fun factor. As long as the suck part of life didn't outweigh the fun part, life was generally pretty damned good.

Somewhere over the surface of the water, I heard an outboard drone. The handful of fishing boats I'd seen arrived just before dawn and headed off around noon. It wasn't enough to justify lifting my head. In a few minutes, they'd drop anchor somewhere, or more accurately, turn on their trolling motors to drift with the current. Then their lines would get wet as they sought some tarpon or bonefish.

After the last seven weeks, I wanted to keep my head buried. My cruising kitty still overflowed, and at the rate I was spending money, I didn't need to work for eight to nine months. That seemed like a decent amount of time. Since I got some unfortunate notoriety recently, a strong possibility existed that some heavy hitters in either the Russian government or even the Bratva might want to put me in their crosshairs. It seemed the more remote I was, the better the chance they'd forget about me. Luckily, the only thing they had was an image, so I was counting on their short memory.

A sharp, buzzing sound echoed across the bay as I slowly lifted my head to take in a different view. A bright white RIB—a rigid inflatable boat—skimmed at speed over the shallow waters of Rabbit Key. It was the kind of dinghy often seen pulled behind luxurious yachts, and its single occupant appeared to be heading for shore to explore the island's trails and pristine beaches. Although no one lived on the small island, it had become popular with campers looking for an overnight stay and a chance to reconnect with nature.

At the sound of a sudden splash, I jumped and whipped my head toward the bow of the boat. A ray feeding in the shallows sliced its wing through the water as if he were trying to imitate a shark. The creature whirled about before vanishing below the surface. A second later, the ray blasted out of the water, its wings spread as if ready to fly away. When it dove back into the sea, my eyes drifted from the frenzied ripples left by the playful ray to the approaching vessel.

The white dinghy had a single male behind the helm. When no warning bells sounded, I lowered my head again. The breeze picked up, and the gathering clouds smelled like rain. Since I knew the foreplay to the precipitation would last longer than the actual downpour, I didn't move.

The hum of the outboard slowed as the driver pulled back on the throttle. He was coming closer, but that wasn't unusual. Somehow, it still made me uncomfortable. I rolled to my side and stared out at the boat coming closer. As he closed the distance, I could almost see the man's face, but the wide-brim hat and dark sunglasses shielded his features.

However, the one thing I could distinguish was the trajectory of the vessel. It bore down on my position without wavering.

As I pointed out, I was currently an undesirable by at least two countries, not to mention a woman with a hefty grudge against me. It was enough to make a man nervous, and I calculated how fast I could get below deck to retrieve my M45 handgun from the forward berth.

Calm down, Gordon. This could just be an extra-amiable fellow out wanting to meet the neighbors. Cruisers often lacked some social boundaries. That was all right, though. Most of the time, they came through in a pinch. Need a tow—a cruiser will waste an entire day dragging a stranger back to the dock. Need some sugar—a cruiser will give you a five-pound bag and show up later with cookies. It was a strange community, and if a neighboring vessel wanted to make friends, I didn't mind. As long as he was a friendly neighbor and not a gung ho assassin intent on putting a bullet in me.

Since I hoped it was the former, it seemed inhospitable to greet the man with a forty-five-caliber pistol in my hand. That kind of thing left a mark on a guy's memory, and it might taint his desire to share should he have those cookies I mentioned earlier.

Despite wanting to appear welcoming, I still rose to my feet. Whoever headed my direction needed to know I was expecting them. People got a little more cautious if they realized I saw they were approaching. Basically, if a man thought he had the element of surprise, he might react bolder and without reservation. Now he knew I saw him coming. There was no catching me off guard.

The outboard slowed as the RIB came within a hundred yards. Despite slowing to idle, the boat's inertia continued it forward. My left hand grabbed the stay that stretched from the top of the mast down to the deck. I moved to the gunwale as the inflatable turned toward the bow.

"Chase?" the driver asked.

I stared at him for a second. "Who are you?" I demanded.

The man smiled. "Sorry, mate," he apologized. He pulled the hat off his head and removed the glasses.

Once revealed, the face was remarkably familiar.

"Milo?" I questioned. "What are you doing out here?"

"Looking for you," the former British spy announced.

I swept my hand down to grab a line coiled on the deck and attached to the midship cleat. "Here," I said, tossing the end to him before moving aft to throw him another line.

Milo Oder tied a perfect hitch knot around his stern cleat. "Can I come aboard?" he asked.

"Of course," I replied, reaching my right arm down to give the older gentleman an assist over the gunwale. "How did you find me?"

The septuagenarian grinned. "An old spy can't give away all his secrets," he suggested. "However, it wasn't the easiest thing. I knew you stopped in Islamorada a week ago, but it took several days to track you here."

"What do you need?"

"I don't," he explained. "Rikki does. She's in a bit of a jam."

2

"I don't have anything fancy," I apologized to the former MI5 agent now sitting across from me in the cockpit of my home.

Milo Oder lifted the icy bottle of Pacifico beer with a grin. "After several hours on the water, a cold cerveza solves most of my problems."

The older man reclined under the shade of my dodger. With the removable vinyl sides down, we enjoyed the benefits of the salty breeze without the sun's sharp rays. I studied the old man, although to call him old was subjective. Milo Oder might have slowed down, but he showed no actual signs of aging. Reminiscent of Dick Clark, the seventy-something-year old appeared to be in his mid-fifties. I'd only met the man once before when I visited his home in a decommissioned lighthouse south of Miami. Oder had a veritable library amassed in the stone building—some of it he acquired during his time in the British Secret Service.

"Have you been motoring between islands all day?" I asked.

"For three days," he admitted. "Normally, there are worse jobs."

"What's going on with Rikki?" I inquired finally.

The gray-haired man sipped his beer for a second. "She disappeared."

I stared at him. Rikki's face flashed through my mind. We hadn't spoken in over a year—or was it two? Time had a way of getting jumbled up when one lived like I did. I often referred to most days of the week as Samesday, since they ran together.

She and I met just south of here in the Keys, and the following weeks became a whirlwind of adventure. Rikki had a knack for trouble, and her passion for treasure hunting caused her to butt heads with all sorts of people. However, the woman took toughness to a different level. One word described her—fearless.

I think Rikki searched as much for her identity as she did for fortune and glory. Her father's aura hung over her. He was, after all, Benjamin Dexter, a world-famous action star of the seventies and eighties. His legacy loomed over her like his movie posters hanging on her walls.

"Tell me about it?" I asked.

Oder explained, "Sam Cornell reached out to me, hoping I could find you."

"No one called the police?" I asked.

"It's complicated," Oder explained.

"With Rikki, that's not a surprise," I said sullenly.

"Sam talked to her father," Oder told me. "Given Rikki's tendencies, he thinks she'll show up in a day or so."

"Let's start with what you know," I demanded. "After that, we fill in the pieces with Sam."

Sam Cornell had been Dexter's trainer during his Hollywood heyday. The man had also been a peer to Oder during the early days of the Troubles in Northern Ireland. Cornell spent his time with the Irish Republic Army trying to free the north from British oppression. On the other side, Oder, tasked by Her Majesty, worked to prevent the secession. I had no idea what in that mix of socio-political gumbo could unite two men in such camaraderie, but they remained steadfast friends.

"My details are mostly about the research I did for her. Rikki reached out to me a few months ago. She'd heard a legend—which, if you'll remember, is all the girl needs to intrigue her. I put out some feelers, and two weeks ago, I got a bite. Of course, I gave the lead to Rikki, and she investigated it."

Milo took another swallow of beer. "Sam says she headed north to some marshy town up there. Somewhere along the coast. She reported the police allegedly arrested her for trespassing."

"That sounds like her," I remarked, remembering her brazen attitude. "Wait, you said 'allegedly.'"

"She sent a message to Sam before they arrested her, but the police say they never encountered her."

I leaned forward. "They didn't arrest her?" I asked.

He shrugged. "Not according to any police records."

"That's some pretty backwoods country up there," I pointed out. "The guys up there don't get a lot of attractive black women wandering off the street."

Milo nodded. "It was something we considered."

For a moment, I stared at the condensation forming on the outside of the bottle of Mexican beer. Droplets formed in the humid air as the cold glass gathered the molecules in the air together before they raced down the side of the bottle.

"Okay, Rikki's a survivor," I announced. "I think you should have called the cops."

"What if the cops did arrest her, though?" Milo asked.

I groaned.

"What was she looking for?" I asked.

"The grave of Useppa," Milo explained.

"Forgive me for my ignorance, but who is Useppa?"

"Have you ever heard the name José Gaspar?"

My head cocked slightly to the right. "The pirate?"

"Right," Oder praised, as if I'd answered the game-winning trivia question. "Gasparilla. The Spanish Scourge."

I nodded. "This isn't the late show," I pointed out.

"It's a bit exciting, though," the historian muttered. "She's hunting down the pirate himself."

"Like his grave?" I questioned.

"No, not really. I guess you could say it's his heart."

"Milo, this doesn't seem to be the best time to romanticize a long-dead pirate," I corrected sternly.

His face soured as I stole the thrill he experienced discussing the buccaneer. I knew little about Gasparilla, except he was a Floridian legend. Many of the islands along the southern coast derived their names from his legend. Every year in Tampa there was a Gasparilla Pirate Festival. Beyond that, he could have discovered Shangri-La, and I would have been clueless.

I understood Milo's excitement. After all, I lived on a boat. The glory days of piracy flowed through my veins. I thought it might have been mandatory to own a pirate flag if a person had a sailboat. *Carina* came with three when I bought her. Although, I rarely flew any of them. While the allure of buccaneering seemed attractive, in reality, most of these men were murderous criminals, raping and pillaging their way across the Caribbean. Not that it differed greatly from the legitimate raping and pillaging done at the will of whatever country's flag a ship flew. Still, the pirate's life promised a certain freedom from the tyranny of corrupt governments and, in most cases, hygiene.

"I thought most of the stories about Gaspar are more legend than history," I commented.

"You are correct," Oder acknowledged. "In fact, there has been no written account about the man ever."

He paused dramatically. "Until now," he exclaimed eerily.

I lifted an eyebrow. "You found something, then?"

"Yes, I traveled to Cuba recently," he told me.

I didn't mention I'd been down there as well. However, with Oder's connections, he might have already known that fact.

"I was researching a few unrelated things, but in the process I did some nosing around for Rikki. I found a letter to Manuel Antonio Valdés Murguía y Saldaña."

"That's quite a name," I remarked.

"The Spanish enjoy a mouthful," Milo quipped. "Valdés published the state-run newspaper for New Spain."

I nodded, waiting for more details to come.

"The correspondence in question came from the viceroy of New Spain, Matias de Gálvez, who mentioned his predecessor's daughter running away with "*azote pirata*" which translates to "pirate scourge."

"That's supposed to be Gaspar?" I asked.

Oder gave me a nod. "The thing about José Gaspar is there is very little written history about him. Almost all of it is legend. In fact, some historians wonder if he might be akin to the Dread Pirate Roberts—just a pseudonym taken by buccaneers and passed on at the end of their career."

"But you don't think that?"

"Chase, if that were the case, we'd have more stories about him. He'd likely have a much longer lifespan in history. That's not what seems to have happened here."

He continued, "Of course, it could be nothing but myth. However, one legend has Gasparilla kidnapping the daughter of Nevada Olivárez, a nobleman from Spain ruling in Mexico City."

"You think this confirms it?"

"It's promising," he remarked. "The interesting part was a reference to sending troops from San Marcos to San Martins."

I stared at Milo for a moment. "You might need to literally draw me a map," I suggested. "I don't know where that's supposed to be."

"San Marcos was the garrison on the St Marks River, near Apalachicola. San Martins likely referred to the St. Martins

River, just north of Tampa. It seems the Spaniards were searching the area for this "scourge pirate."

"Knowing Rikki, I guess she didn't wait a day before she hauled ass up there?" I asked.

"More or less," Oder agreed. "She sailed her yacht up the coast."

"*Talitha*," I commented, remembering the name of Rikki's sixty-five-foot Nomad.

Oder nodded, saying, "I don't know how long it took her. However, she'd been there a few days, digging through historical records and exploring the waterways. Then, Sam gets a text that a couple of cops showed up in the woods. She figured they were going to fine her for trespassing. Apparently, she had crossed an archaeological dig. After that, she was silent."

I leaned forward. What Milo left me with was a sick feeling in my gut. Rikki was a capable woman, but if she'd been running silent for days now, the likely reason was she was alligator bait.

"Dammit," I mumbled. "Where did she anchor *Talitha*?"

"Sam's got the coordinates," Oder admitted.

"Are you coming with me?" I questioned. "Or do you need to head back to shore?"

His face went slack. "You're leaving now?"

"It's about 250 miles north. If I sail straight through, I can do it in a little over twenty-four hours. With any luck, I can shave a few hours off."

"I guess I need to head back then," Oder remarked. I wondered what he expected me to do when he came here.

Feasibly, I could sail *Carina* back to Islamorada and dock her there, then rent a car or something to head north. However, that alone would eat up ten to twelve hours. I was only a few miles from the open Gulf, and if I stayed offshore away from the shallower shelf that ran along the western coast of Florida, I could travel a little faster. Although I'd be fighting the current coming out of the Gulf, the wind was coming from the west.

My Tartan moved quickly when it was on a beam reach, with the breeze perpendicular to the vessel.

"Can I help you do anything?" Milo asked.

While the sentiment was appreciated, I had a rhythm for doing things, and a novice like Milo only slowed things down.

"No, I got it," I explained, as I ducked below deck.

"You can get those coordinates from Sam," I added, hoping to give him some task. Besides, once he and I separated, I'd have no way of communicating with either Milo or Sam. I didn't have a cellphone on board *Carina*. The only communication I had was a VHF radio and a Single Side Band radio. They worked great for communicating on the water, and they didn't get random spam calls in the middle of my naps.

"How will you sail that long?" Milo asked. "Won't you need some rest?"

"Once I get offshore, I have an auto pilot and radar. The radar alerts me if anything gets in my way. I'll catnap some."

He set his beer down. "Do you have a pen and paper?" he asked. "I have those coordinates."

"Hang on," I announced, returning through the companionway. Keying the touchscreen on my chartplotter, I said, "Give it to me."

He rattled off the latitude and longitude as I tapped it into my navigation computer. Once the screen showed the destination, I saved the waypoint.

"I guess you don't need me," Milo muttered.

"I'll be underway in about half an hour," I explained. "You can tell Sam that I'm on my way."

He nodded as he moved to the gunwale. As he climbed down into the dinghy, he glanced up at me. "Find her, Chase," he pleaded.

3

The weather did not remain cooperative, which was usually the case when I was on a tight schedule. Timetables meant nothing to the cruising gods, whoever they were. The breeze shifted directions about six hours after I hit the Gulf. Over the next twelve hours, *Carina* slogged into a headwind against the current. After a while, I surrendered, furled the genoa sail, and fired up the motor.

Like I told Milo, the autopilot did most of the work. I took a wide arc away from shore to avoid fishing charters and cruisers trying to cling to the coastline. It didn't eliminate all the traffic, but it reduced it down. The closest any vessel came to me was about six miles. The radar pinged the freighter and pulled me out of a doze. Once I assured myself we were clear of each other, I fell back on the cockpit cushions and watched the waves go past.

A few of the quick catnaps stretched as long as an hour and a half. Resting was sometimes a luxury when the Corps deployed me overseas. My body learned to take whatever sleep it could get. If the conditions were perfect, I could lean against a post and nap on my feet. Which meant eight or nine naps worked as well, if not better, than a full night in the rack.

"Motor Vessel *Talitha*, this is Sailing Vessel *Carina*, come in," I called over the VHF radio when I first spotted the Nomad yacht several miles off the bow.

It was the middle of the afternoon, and I was eager to drop anchor. The sooner I made contact with Sam Cornell, the quicker I began my search for Rikki.

When Sam Cornell came over from Ireland in the eighties, he gravitated to Hollywood, where his experience transitioned him into the movie world. Soon, he met Benjamin Dexter, and the two developed a relationship. Sam trained Dexter, who was notorious for doing his own stunts, to fight like a soldier on-screen. When Dexter's film career waned, he kept Sam on. Now, the former IRA soldier and stuntman acted as a steward aboard *Talitha*. The effort was a poorly disguised attempt to offer protection for Rikki as she traversed the globe following history. Rikki long ago proved herself capable of handling adversity, and Sam seemed to understand that, operating more like a mentor than a protector for the woman.

"This is *Talitha*," a voice responded.

"*Talitha*, can you switch over to channel twenty?" I asked. On the water, the Coast Guard preferred mariners to use channel sixteen for contact only. Once a vessel responded, protocol suggested moving to a less populated frequency for conversation.

"Roger," the response came.

After adjusting the frequency, I said, "Sam, this is Chase."

"Chase," the voice replied in a brogue. "Good to hear ya."

"How is the holding there?" I asked. "I want to drop the hook off your bow."

Sam Cornell answered, "We're sitting in twelve feet of water. The bottom is nice and sandy, too."

"Roger," I acknowledged. That was a perfect depth—exactly what the charts suggested it would be. The tide was going out, but it should stay around ten to eleven feet.

After adjusting the heading with the autopilot, I began lowering the mainsail, letting the motor push us for the time being. Once I reached *Talitha*, the covers shrouded the sails to protect them from the ultraviolet rays, and I'd coiled the sheets and halyards neatly. I switched off the autopilot, taking control of the helm. The wind came from the west now that I was almost to my destination. Such was the way of sailing. Generally, when cruising, it was best to have a tentative plan so that when the weather stuck it to me, I can adjust. That attitude made it difficult to maintain a schedule. Usually I could pick a destination to reach or a time frame, but rarely did both line up.

As I spun the wheel, the bow nosed into the wind, and I pulled back on the throttle. I could operate the anchor windlass from the cockpit. A clunk-clunk-clunk of the chain feeding out of the anchor locker reverberated through the hull, and I felt the vibrations all the way in the back of the Tartan. The rode, the length of chain between the ground tackle and the vessel, stretched out. A display on the helm measured the length in feet, and when the scope reached fifteen feet, I shut the windlass off, shifted the diesel motor into reverse, and gently backed up. The result dug the plow anchor deep into the sand.

Slipping the motor back into neutral, I fed out more scope until the digital display indicated thirty-two feet stretched from the hook to the bow. That length allowed *Carina* to swing if the wind or seas shifted. Most of the time, the boat found its direction and pulled the rode tight. Any cruiser's worst nightmare was having an anchor drag. It was one of those things that happened to everyone, but we were all annoyed and embarrassed by it, as if it passed judgment on us as sailors. I'd had it happen twice in the Bahamas. Luckily, Carina never bumped another boat, although in Stanley Cay she was about ten inches off a fifty-five-foot Carver when I got on deck. Red-faced, I moved her away from the motor yacht while the owners watched me with hands on their hips.

"Chase," the VHF squawked.

"Go ahead," I called.

"Why don't you come on over?" Sam offered. "I can put together a bite to eat."

"Roger that," I said. It was the next thing on my agenda anyway, but Sam Cornell stood on principle and the offering was requisite.

My dinghy was a gray RIB I'd bought a year ago to replace the one I'd lost off Costa Rica. Compared to my old one, *Beth*, this little vessel was much newer, more efficient, and far more boring. I never named her because she was so nondescript. On the other hand, *Beth* had been a handcrafted wooden boat I'd revived from the dead. She had a colorful hull, and while she bounced a bit more than this one, she did so with style and grace. The rubber pontoons on this one absorbed the shock, but the stretched vinyl never felt like a real boat.

Talitha sat two hundred feet off the starboard side of *Carina*. The motor rumbled to life, and I twisted the throttle just past idle and puttered toward the big yacht. If I'd still had *Beth*, this would have been close enough to row over. The rigid inflatable lacked the v-bottom, which would have made it easy to slice through the water. Instead, the rounded tubes skimmed over the surface, and rowing a boat like that was more difficult.

The rubber hull bumped up over the swim platform jutting off the stern of the sixty-five-foot Nomad SUV. Sam Cornell stepped from the aft deck and caught the dinghy's painter as I tossed it to him. He coiled it around a cleat with a hitch knot.

"Permission to come aboard?" I asked.

"Yes," the Irishman responded. He motioned for me to follow him, and I grabbed the handrail before hoisting myself up to the deck.

"Any word?" I questioned, as we moved through the glass doors into the salon.

"Nothing yet."

I'd forgotten that I would be face-to-face with four versions of Benjamin Dexter glaring down at me in all their glory. The vintage movie posters showed a much younger version of Dexter, but if you stared into his eyes, it was easy to see the resemblance between Dexter and Rikki. Of course, Rikki's beauty seemed flawless while Benjamin Dexter's felt structured.

Sam Cornell didn't take long to put together a meal. He had a spread of crab salad with toasted baguettes and fresh fruit.

"Have a seat," he offered, and I obliged.

"Thank you, Sam," I said as I took a slice of bread and scooped some shellfish onto it.

"It surprised me Milo found you so quickly," he admitted.

I glanced up at him. "Why did you come looking for me?" I asked. "There had to be a faster route."

He shrugged. "I'm working all the angles," he told me. "While I didn't get to know you before, Rikki spoke highly of you."

The first and last time I saw Rikki, Sam spent most of the time in a hospital, where he recovered from a near-fatal attack. We met briefly when he got out of the doctors' care, but the man was going to stay with a niece while he healed.

"It's likely undeserved," I remarked.

"You pulled up anchor and came running as soon as you heard she was in trouble," Sam pointed out. "That confirms a lot of it."

I chewed a bite slowly. Sam Cornell had a bloody history, and I stewed for a brief minute about how blunt to be. Raw felt like the best course.

"It's been too many days," I said. "The odds of finding her safe aren't great."

He nodded. His voice saddened as he remarked, "I know. If I didn't have to stumble around with that damned cane half the time, I'd head into those woods and find whatever was left of her. Whoever hurt her would face my wrath."

My eyes shifted to the wooden cane leaning against the cabinet by the door. He hadn't used it since I came aboard, but he'd had the railing along the steps and aft deck to support him. The injuries he sustained in the attack last year left his leg shattered in several spots.

"You want revenge?" I asked.

"Or answers," he replied. "I want her to be safe and back on board. If she's not, I want to hurt the person responsible for it."

"She could have gotten injured in the wild," I pointed out. "It could be no one's fault."

"She messaged me," he explained, pulling his phone from his left pocket.

The device slid across the table face up, and I read the message, "Cops are here."

The next message said, "Probably going to arrest me for trespassing."

That was all. There were several messages from Sam asking if she was safe. Then he begged her to answer.

"Her phone lost signal after that," he said.

My brow furrowed. "What do you mean?"

"She has a tracking app on her phone. It stopped transmitting not long after that. It could mean the phone lost power. If the phone was turned on, I should be able to activate with a PIN, but so far nothing."

"That might happen if it's at the bottom of the sea," I suggested.

"Could be," he admitted. "The point was people were there with her. She thought they were policemen, but I called the local departments. No one has a record of Rikki Talens. Whoever they were, they didn't arrest her."

"You know where her phone lost signal?"

Sam nodded. He reached behind him and retrieved an iPad. After the device registered his face, he rotated the tablet, so I had a better view. A red arrow flashed over a satellite map. The indicator was in the middle of the Suwannee River, just south of a small, wooded island.

"Certainly doesn't bode well," I suggested. "The last signal came before it went into the water. How did she get out there?"

"The dinghy," Sam answered.

"Has anyone found it?"

The Irishman shook his head. No surprise. Even though dinghies had a hull identification number, they didn't get checked a lot. It was an easy resale item. The chances of a Florida Fish and Wildlife agent running the HIN were virtually zero unless an actual crime was involved. I guessed the boat had its up-to-date registration still affixed to the hull. Until that expired, the new owner wouldn't have to think about registering it. Sure, it was illegal not to do so, but it wasn't uncommon to be tooling around the bay with the previous owner's registration number.

It was a little over twelve miles from *Talitha* to the pin on the map—if I could travel in a straight line. Unfortunately, the river wound through the Florida wilds, and I bet that doubled the time. It would be a two-hour ride just to get to the location. That wouldn't give me long to search before dark.

"I'll have to camp," I told Sam. "That gives me time to get there before sunset, and first thing in the morning, I can start searching."

"You'll need some gear," he pointed out.

"I have plenty of camping stuff on board *Carina*," I explained.

He stood up slowly. His right leg straightened as if he were testing to make sure it worked before putting any weight on it. Once he assured himself that the appendage would hold, he ambled toward the galley.

"Here," he announced, tossing me a sat phone. "I hear you abhor the damned things, but at least I can track you, too."

I caught the phone with my right hand before shoving the last bite of bread and crab salad into my mouth.

"There's not much time," I said with a mouthful. "I'll be heading upriver in half an hour."

Sam's chin dipped curtly, and I stood from the table. Across the water, I could see the village of Suwannee that sat at the mouth of the river. Beyond the small town lay hundreds of square miles of forest. Somewhere in there, I hoped Rikki was still alive.

4

I awoke to a buzzing sound. My head lifted from the bottom of the dinghy. After pushing away the cloth I'd rigged over me, I stared out into the night. As soon as the cover moved, mosquitoes swarmed around my face. I dropped the fabric and rummaged for some bug spray. It wouldn't matter much to these bastards. Florida bugs weren't like insects elsewhere. They thrived on citronella and DEET. When I was anchored offshore, the breeze prevented them from taking over. However, inland, only a few miles from the Gulf, the mosquitoes built a society intent on devouring every drop of blood in my body.

The buzz continued. It was an outboard—at least I thought. Definitely some kind of motor.

Inside my head, there was a little clock that was usually accurate to within ten minutes. Right now, it let me know it was almost four in the morning.

Fisherman, I told myself. Those guys kept the worst hours.

I lay back in the dinghy's bottom. Despite arriving with plenty of daylight to set up camp, I opted to sleep on the water. Dense woods covered the island about a hundred feet from me. I didn't mind clearing the area, but I'd be pushing it to pitch a tent before dusk rolled around. By anchoring out a way, I hoped no curious wildlife would climb aboard. Sleeping on the fiberglass floor wasn't the most comfortable, but I'd slept in a lot worse places. At least in the bottom of the inflatable, the gently rocking and swaying of the boat reminded me of *Carina*.

The sky glistened with stars. With no moon out, the constellations exploded across the dark expanse. Most people consider camping out a quiet, peaceful event. However, on the wild western coast of Florida, it was louder than Times Square. The trees squawked, chirped, buzzed, groaned, and howled at decibels that astounded me. At one point in the night, I stirred awake at the sound of a large growl followed by a huffing. A panther somewhere on the other side of the river.

Now, though, the buzzing motor came closer. I felt the butt of my M45, nestled under my right leg. My biggest concern was a wayward alligator finding the dinghy interesting. Of course, when I heard the panther's warning cry, it occurred to me to be worried a little about it, too. It was a misconception that big cats didn't swim, and a small inflatable raft might make an ideal resting point for a panther to stop.

It wasn't a great worry on my part. The fact was, I was more likely to fall victim to a venomous snake bite before I had to battle an alligator and a panther playing king of the island with my boat.

My eyes slid closed, and I listened to the din of droning insects dissipate as the motor grew louder. No, it wasn't just one motor. There were two distinct pitches echoing over the water. It wasn't the sound of a dual engine boat. Even with two outboards running on the back of a boat, the engines tended to sync up. Perhaps that was because of their proximity to each other. I wasn't sure. But this was two separate boats. They were together, but not next to each other. More like one was following the other.

The noise grew closer as they rounded a bend to the west of my location. Now, I was positive they didn't sound like regular outboards, and when the drivers slowed, my brain clicked. The motor sounds paired up with something in the database of my head. It was some kind of personal watercraft—a Sea-Doo or WaveRunner. I knew those high-pitched reports from quiet anchorages where some dumbass buzzed by *Carina* too close for comfort. Unlike a lot of cruisers, it wasn't the vehicle itself I hated; the damned drivers were the problem. Actually, I loved racing around on those "water motorcycles"—the high speeds and tight turns. They were a blast if one showed proper respect to others. Of course, those nightmare PWC drivers tended to be nightmares in all things.

A rolling wave lifted the dinghy as the PWCs' wake motored past me.

"What the hell is that?" a male voice shouted with a thick rural accent.

"Campers?" a response came.

I tightened my grip on the forty-five-caliber pistol. These two were probably nothing more than local rednecks. I'd come across a few in my time. They didn't appreciate visitors rolling through their state.

Through the cloth covering me, I saw a beam of light shoot over the boat and aim toward the shore.

"I don't see no one," the first voice remarked.

"Probably up in the trees," the second commented.

"Damn," the first said. It sounded like "dayum." He continued, "We gotta go up in 'ere, don't we?"

"Let's swing back through later," the second suggested.

"Wanna take the boat?" the first asked. "I bet we could sell that."

"No, maybe they'll move along in the morning."

"Be easier to stomp through the grass in the daylight, too," the first one agreed somewhat reluctantly.

"C'mon, Jace," the second demanded.

The PWCs roared away. The resulting waves pitched the dinghy about like a cork. After a minute, the tumultuous surface calmed to a gentle rocking. The whine of the motors faded as they headed toward the Gulf.

It seemed like these guys might reappear later with less than hospitable intentions. I doubted a couple of Florida backwoods boys were anything to lose sleep over, but now I was fully awake. I could drift back to sleep for a bit, but my mind churned. Would those two know anything about Rikki?

If they were true to their word, I could expect them back. It might be a good time to ask them about her.

For the next hour, I let my eyes close, but sleep stayed just out of reach. I wanted to get to shore and look around. Much like Jace, though, I preferred waiting until the sun was up. I'd just as soon not startle a sleeping gator when I could wait until he woke up.

The next hour ticked by slowly. Sometime before dawn, the constant chirping of insects died off. The first few tweets and caws of the early birds out hunting for their worms echoed through the trees. I waited another ten minutes before pushing the cloth back. The early morning sky turned a mixture of purple and pink as the sun prepared to come up.

I groaned as I hauled myself up from the hard floor of the dinghy, feeling my back creak with soreness. I scanned the shore, taking in the lush foliage of the tall trees and carpet of greenery that lined the banks of the river.

The air was humid and still like all parts of Florida that are more than a mile from the shoreline. I noticed a hint of decay floating above the surface and something sweet that tickled my nose.

A sudden splash behind me interrupted the calm, sending a white crane flapping above the water. Whatever creature caused the commotion disappeared under the surface again by the time I twisted around to locate it.

Somewhere out here, Rikki vanished. My gut warned me that there was very little chance of finding her alive. I wondered about the two good ole boys that came by earlier. They didn't sound completely harmless, and it wasn't unheard of in some of the backwater parts of Florida for the locals to cause trouble for visitors. They resented people skating in on their kayaks and paddleboards to disrupt their hunting and fishing grounds.

Those types seemed to spread across America—low-income citizens struggling to just live off the land. Yet, some city-slicker came through to take their fish and deer for mere sport.

I wondered if they'd seen Rikki. It wasn't fair to judge them too quickly, but this section of Florida was rural. A pretty African-American woman might seem easy prey to some people. Rumors swirled that there was still Klan activity in these parts. Hatred like theirs was dangerous. Individually, a person might think better about some actions. Clump those same folks together, though, under their righteous cause, and the collective common sense plummetted. It was difficult to condemn, or even stop, insanity when the crowd was against you.

Of course, I knew Rikki, and if she ran into a few country boys with ill intent, she might inflict enough damage to make them rethink.

I towed the ten-pound anchor into the dinghy, letting the rope coil on the floor. There wasn't much point in starting the motor, so I paddled to the shore. After pulling the inflatable up on the muddy bank, I stepped into the trees to relieve myself.

The little island in the middle of the river was called Turkey Island on the map. Generally, those names didn't mean much. Perhaps, many years ago, this little chunk of mud was rife with turkeys. At the moment, I didn't see any species of birds, although several chirped and tweeted in the trees.

If Rikki came up the river, this would have been a suitable spot to come ashore. Sawgrass and foxtails covered the riverbank along the northern shore of Turkey Island. Swaths of green pressed against the mud where boats regularly pulled ashore.

Sharp blades gnawed at my legs as I waded through the two-foot-tall growth. The early morning dew was drying quickly off the leaves as the sun began baking the forest. This was going to be a hot one, not unusual in the Sunshine State, but I preferred to be close enough to the coast to get the sea breeze. Here the only wind came up the river, and the vegetation along the banks kept it funneled over the river. Sweat had already appeared on my forehead, and before long, I might risk the brown water of the Suwannee for a respite.

One of the first warnings I ever got came from Randy, the harbor master at the Tilly Marina. He advised me to stay out of any water that looked like iced tea. "Anything deeper than six inches has a sixty percent chance of having a gator lurking at the bottom," he explained.

I doubted the accuracy of his statistics, but most natives assumed something similar. Granted, most alligators scurried away from a guy my size, but there were a few out there that wouldn't strain a muscle to drag me down to the bottom. Even smaller ones might mistake a finger or toe for a tasty snack they could fit in their mouth. Little teeth hurt, too.

The island only comprised about two acres, and I crossed through the middle. Maple and birch trees towered above me, decorated with tresses of Spanish moss. The canopy shielded the sun from me, and amid the trees, the temperature dropped about ten degrees.

In the distance, I heard the familiar whines of the personal watercraft that had visited this morning. Two minutes later, the sound came closer until the RPMs dropped suddenly. I envisioned the two pulling up beside my dinghy. For a second, I considered heading back toward them, but I continued across the island, looking for any clues that Rikki had stopped.

I counted three sites where someone had built a small campfire. None of those campsites appeared to be recent. Bits of litter was scattered along the ground in each of the three blackened areas. Most of the trash had disintegrated in the weather.

Tracking people through the wild wasn't one of my strengths. Jay Delp could follow a squirrel around a state park, but my skills lent themselves to the "point and shoot" variety.

I could, however, tiptoe through the woods—something which Jace and his friend weren't capable of. The tramping through brush and trees announced them long before they came into sight. I sank into the brush, waiting to see how they reacted.

Thirty seconds later, the two came into view. Both men were gaunt and small framed. Neither wore a shirt, leading me to guess they were local in the woods. Most people would protect their skin from the onslaught of mosquitoes. These boys, who were barely mid-twenties, had grown accustomed to the bites. The whites of their eyes were wide, and my initial reaction warned me they might be high—another reason the incessant bug bites might not annoy them.

Both men had dirty blond hair and day-old scraggly beards. They had a similar enough appearance to make me think they were related. The one in the front held a two-foot machete out. In the rear, the second man had a cheap twenty-two-caliber pistol hanging off the belt of his cutoff jeans.

Where I was hiding, the two couldn't see me. It confirmed they might be under some influence. My cover wasn't good enough to fool most people, but these two glanced my way twice without noticing me.

Steel pressed against my lower back, reassuring me that the M45 was within reach.

"They must be around here," the guy in the rear mumbled.

"Yeah, they moved the boat," Machete remarked.

I rested on my haunches and watched.

Machete twirled the blade with some faux panache as he sliced through several branches. The angle of his swipe was acute, and while the blade was sharp, it didn't cut through the limbs. Instead, the weight bent them at their fulcrum, letting the leaves dangle toward the dirt.

With my hand on the butt of my gun, I raised up after the two passed me.

"Hello," I exclaimed. "I wasn't expecting company."

Both men spun around, surprised.

"What are you doing here?" Machete growled.

The second man snapped his wrist to bring the twenty-two out of his holster. It was a practiced move, but he had far from mastered it. The M45 came around my side and leveled with the sights trained on his chest. The revolver in his hand was barely off his hip. Instinctively, he came up with it.

"I wouldn't," I advised. "This is a forty-five. The impact will knock you off your feet before you can get a clean shot off. Maybe the twenty-two will drop me right away. Or it won't. In which case, I can get at least another shot off. Or more."

My eyes shifted to Machete, and I offered him a smirk.

Behind me, I heard a distinctive chunk of a pump-action shotgun.

"I'm pretty sure I can cut you in half before either of them hits the ground," a deep voice drawled behind me.

My head turned slightly to see a graying man in his fifties pointing a twelve-gauge Browning double-barrel shotgun at my head. I let my grip loosen on the M45. Machete stepped forward and grabbed it from my hand.

"Listen guys, I'm just exploring the river," I explained. "I wasn't looking for any trouble."

The older man turned the shotgun in a smooth arc before thrusting the butt into the side of my head.

5

The blackness faded about the time I landed in the bottom of my inflatable dinghy. Despite the inflated chambers, the floor had one-inch-thick fiberglass floor for stability. Since I'd pulled the boat up on shore, when I hit, face-first, in the boat, it was like taking a face-plant into the decking.

I remained limp, a feat made easier by the fact I was only barely conscious. Crumpled on the floor of the RIB, I evaluated the situation.

"That motor's worth a couple of grand," one of the younger two pointed out.

"I don't need a damned motor," the older man with the Browning spouted off. "Take him out and sink the boat. By the time they find him, he'll be gator bait."

"Hell, yeah," one remarked. I think he was the one with the rusted twenty-two.

My wrists were bound behind my back. With slight movements, I tested the binds. String—haystring or some kind of hemp. identical twine bound my ankles together, too.

"Make sure he doesn't have any ID," Browning ordered. "Don't make it too easy for them to identify him."

Someone climbed into the boat as the other pushed the RIB off the shore. The boat rocked as the river's current caught the stern. No one else jumped aboard. If they intended on sinking me in some deep part of the river, the driver needed a way back. Whichever of the two young thugs wasn't in the dinghy with me would be following on a PWC.

The outboard on the RIB roared to life, and the gentle bobbing along the surface stopped as the engine pressed us over the surface. There wasn't much chance of me breaking the string on my wrists before the driver noticed me. I need to wrestle control of the situation away from him, but to do that, I needed to remind him I wasn't a threat. For most people, being hog-tied on the bottom of a boat was a far cry from being a threat. Even now, he had the advantage. If I took a misstep, he might just shoot me here.

I started with a groan and a twist. It was supposed to appear like I was trying to get myself up, but the rope left me unable to move. What it actually did was allow me to rotate my head away from the driver. I blinked slowly, letting him think I was just coming to. Machete steered the boat atop the back of the starboard pontoon. The wooden handle of the blade stuck up over his right shoulder, where it hung from a sheath across his back. He tucked my forty-five under his belt like a trophy. Off the stern, I saw Twenty-Two trailing behind on a Yamaha WaveRunner. It was an older model, but it seemed to run fine.

"What are you doing?" I asked.

"Don't try anything," he warned.

I gave a struggle against the rope—a show of how incapacitated I was.

"Look, I didn't mean anything," I said. "People will be looking for me."

He cocked his head and stared at me. The unspoken words were either "Tough shit" or something along the lines of "Good luck to them." Of course, I was guessing. I wobbled on my butt until I was sitting up.

"Are you going to kill me?"

"Of course not," he lied.

If Rikki ran into these guys, they might have done the same thing to her. She could be at the bottom of the river now.

"Listen, I was searching for a friend who is missing. She came through here several days ago."

"Ain't seen nobody."

"She's an African-American woman. Very attractive."

He shook his head.

"Her father is crazy rich. He'd pay a lot of money to get her back."

He didn't react. At least for a second.

"How rich is he?"

"Do you know who Benjamin Dexter is?"

Machete's brow furrowed. "The guy from those robot movies?"

I thought for a second. Movies weren't my specialty. "Yeah, that's him."

Suddenly, his demeanor changed. The prospect intrigued him. "If I knew where she was, how much would he pay?"

"Dude's worth like a hundred million," I told him, pulling a number wildly out of my ass. "How much do you think he'd pay to get his daughter back safely?"

Machete considered this, and I twisted my wrists, trying to loosen up the rope. It wasn't likely that I'd free myself, but if I could give my hands some movement, that would help.

"A million dollars?" he asked.

I shrugged. "Guess it depends on what happened to her," I pointed out. "Do you know where she is?"

"We didn't do anything to her," he stated, glancing back at his partner behind us.

He never said he didn't know where she was, only that they did nothing to her. There was something telling in that statement.

"Tell me where she is, and I'll make sure you get the reward."

He stole another peek over his shoulder at the WaveRunner. His mind was simple to read. Would he have to share with his partners?

I watched as something clicked in his eyes.

"Benjamin Dexter, right?" he asked, as his gaze settled on something ahead of us.

My head turned to a wide spot in the river. The current appeared to slow, a sign the water might be deeper here. Deep water wasn't good for me.

"Is he here?" Machete asked me with some anticipation.

I cocked my head. "Here? In Florida? No."

"I'm sure I can find him," he commented.

My head shook. "Have you ever tried to reach out to a celebrity? You need to actually have their number."

Machete nodded in agreement. "I'm sure his daughter can give it to me."

I squirmed around a bit. "Look, if I don't come back and you offer her up, they'll assume you had something to do with my death," I said as I inched my feet up under me.

"Naw," he refuted. "I don't think they'll miss you."

My stare moved over his shoulder for a second, and I winced.

It was a stupid trick humans have been playing since time began. "Made you look," we would taunt when the gimmick played out.

Machete fell for it, turning his head to follow my line of sight.

"Arrgg!" I grunted, shoving up off the bottom of the boat with my feet.

The pounce was awkward, but I kept my target locked. My right shoulder caught Machete in the side. He rocked back as all my weight pummeled him. We struck the water, and I kicked my feet—mermaid-style since they were still bound. We sank several feet, and I rolled backward, pulling my arms over my ass and legs. My wrists rotated around as I got them over my feet.

I looked up at the surface, where a silhouette struggled above me. Kicking up, I grabbed Machete by the waist of his shorts and jerked him under the water again. As we dove, I twisted around so the constant swirl disoriented him. My arms wrapped around his throat, pulling him down.

Despite several attempts, I couldn't get the leverage to break his neck, and the man thrashed. A weird pop sounded under water, ringing through my ear drums. He had the M45 in his hand as he struggled to shoot at me.

Like the alligators that lived in these waters, I spun Machete around like it was a death roll. Every time I wrenched him one way and back the other, he struggled to hold on to the gun.

My lungs burned. He'd gotten to the surface for a breath before I tugged him back under, but I was still working off the mouthful I swallowed before going overboard. I counted on my stamina to last longer than his, even though I was exerting more energy.

Another gunshot rippled through the water, ringing my ears. I couldn't stand it much longer. My arms came from around his throat, and my right hand grabbed the handle of the machete.

The man had gone limp, and I pushed up with my feet toward the surface. It seemed like we were about fifteen feet down, and the swim toward the surface felt interminable. When my head broke the surface, I swallowed a lungful of air before sinking quickly back down. On the way under, I glimpsed the WaveRunner moving in wide circles about two hundred feet away from me.

My ears continued to ring from the gunshot, and I couldn't hear the PWCs engine, even underwater where all sound was amplified. The gunshots, so close to me, left my auditory sense dazed.

Quickly, I cut the binds on my wrist and hands before swimming for the other shore. I took a chance to surface for a second to grab some air and figure out which way to head. By the time I submerged again, I estimated the distance to shore was about 150 feet. Easy enough swim—as long as I didn't run into anything bigger than me in the water.

When the depth shallowed to a couple of feet, I rolled to my back in the mud, letting just my face break the surface. I took in several slow, deep breaths as I scanned the river. Pistol Boy stood on his WaveRunner making swaths around the river. He'd lost track of where we went in, but he still searched desperately for his partner.

Debris littered the shoreline, and I kept my head obscured by a mass of flotsam. The same tall sawgrass covered the riverbank. When the WaveRunner turned again toward the other bank, I slithered through the mud like a snake into the grass. A few feet from me, something shuffled, moving blades of grass.

Every muscle in my body froze as I waited. I still couldn't hear anything except the ringing in my ears.

I watched through the gaps of green grass as the blond kid on the WaveRunner shouted at the water a few hundred feet from where I lay hidden on the shoreline. The smell of soured mud filled my nostrils, and I waited. The inflatable dinghy was over a quarter of a mile down the river, having continued on its track after I hit the water.

Fifteen minutes passed, and the kid, who had collapsed onto the handlebars for the last ten minutes, finally sat up. He fished in his pocket, pulling out a phone. The WaveRunner's engine idled, and the PWC floated with the current toward the sea.

I still couldn't hear him as he talked, but after a minute, he slammed his fist into the rubber between the handles. He returned the phone to his pocket before squeezing the throttle. I watched him stop alongside the dinghy.

Slowly, I raised up, watching down the river as the kid dragged the inflatable out into the middle. He must have sliced the pontoons. The gray rubber sank out of sight, and the ten-horsepower motor dragged the rest to the riverbed.

Another movement in the grass a few feet away caused me to raise the machete in my hand. I inched forward and peered through the brush.

A four-foot alligator stared up at me with an open mouth. My eyes cut to the side, and I took a big step away as the little beast hissed at me. When I was far enough back, I relaxed. He might not eat me alive, but his teeth were razor sharp and, no doubt, filled with bacteria. He could bite me and wait for sepsis to kill me.

I climbed up the bank into the woods before turning back. Pistol Boy and the WaveRunner were gone, having headed back up the river.

The satellite phone and rations were in the dinghy. My forty-five sat at the bottom of the river. It was ten miles back to the Gulf—as the crow flies. However, following the river it would probably be a bit more.

I had nothing.

Except questions. What did these boys have out here worth killing me over?

Given how Machete reacted, did he know where Rikki was?

6

"How the hell did this happen, Tommy?" Gray asked.

"I don't know," Tommy exclaimed. "I was following on the WaveRunner. Next thing I see is the guy and Jace falling over the back of the boat."

"Fuck!" Gray cursed. "We tied him up."

Tommy nodded vigorously. "He was still out when we threw him in the boat."

Gray shook his head slowly. He watched his son closely. "You're sure Jace didn't come up?"

"Dad, I circled the river for half an hour before I called you."

"He could have gotten to shore," Gray suggested.

Tommy shook his head. "He'd have waved me down."

Gray's shoulders sank. "I don't care. Get back out there. Jace is tough; he might still be out there."

"Dad..."

"Don't," Gray snapped. "I told you what to do. Send a couple of guys out on the side-by-sides. They can search the riverbanks. If Jace got out, he'd be coming back on the north side."

Tommy Connors nodded slowly. "Are you going to tell her?"

Gray's eyes narrowed. "The fuck you think I'm going to do—just ignore it? Hope she doesn't notice her oldest son doesn't come to dinner anymore?"

"I couldn't do anything about it," Tommy declared.

Gray growled, but conceded. "The big guy didn't make it either?"

"I heard one of them surface, but by the time I turned around, they were gone again."

"How the hell does a guy trussed up like a calf take out your brother?"

Tommy didn't answer. He had several thoughts, but nothing he said would appease Gray.

Gray Connors was a harsh, domineering figure. Despite his graying temples, the man still stood broad like a farmhand. His biceps bulged through the short-sleeved shirts he wore. He had the undeniable appearance that warned anyone who saw him to give him a wide berth.

And for the most part, everyone in the western part of the county recognized the man for what he was. The patriarch of the family that had its hands in everything. It was a county that offered little to the state. The only major cities were thirty miles from the Connorses.

The Connors family name stretched back a hundred years or more. The family history dictated that Gray's great-great-grandfather worked the riverboats until the railroads turned them obsolete. He landed in a small community called Clay's Landing. When the paddleboats vanished, the town slowly faded away.

Like so many people, the Connorses found a different kind of employ—bootlegging and smuggling. It was often under the guise of fishing, but they imported rum from Cuba through the twenties. According to Gray's grandfather, Wilson Connors, who held the office of governor in the early twentieth century, had a standing order for a case of Cuban rum every month. Wilson Connors joked that no one gave a shit what happened in the backwoods of Florida, and if Al Capone had moved his business down to Steinhatchee, the man would have retired at a ripe old age.

After Prohibition ended, the Connorses continued smuggling contraband up the western coast of Florida and right up the Suwanee. Illegal rum turned into marijuana and opium. When Gray connected with the cartels, the money really began to flow up the river. Gray continued to cultivate his contacts throughout the Southeast. Most of what he brought up from Mexico was heroin, but recently, he'd begun shipping out an equally valuable commodity—women. Actually, it was mostly teenage girls. Most were runaways who thought Florida would offer some escape. Luckily, his supplier could handle the goods he offered.

The best part was that the spoils of their business never seemed obvious. This land they owned was worthless—nowhere close to anything the tourists wanted to see. Even the state land had fallen into some disrepair, leaving swaths of forest ignored by the bureaucrats. Now, this section of coast was often skipped over by pleasure craft as the water in the Gulf of Mexico remained too shallow for bigger yachts to cross through. Most cruising boats jumped around the bend in what Gray called Florida's armpit.

The truth was that Gray spent a great deal of energy ensuring the county remained worthless. He fought investors wanting to bring in fishing resorts and natural eco-tours. If the area remained locked in the fifties era, no one would pay it much attention.

That also meant keeping the citizens happy. The median income of the county was below the poverty line because Connors made certain the people there didn't need anything. No one missed a meal because three times a year, a trailer of livestock arrived at Charlie's Deer Processor—all off the books and never during deer season. When Charlie finished butchering everything, anyone was welcome to stock up their freezers. It was all done by word of mouth.

Visitors were discouraged—something that continued to grow more difficult. People were growing tired of crowds, especially over the last few years. The internet didn't help either. Someone might slip in and take a picture of one of the cenotes in the area, post it to Instagram, and suddenly, twenty-something kids showed up in their Jeeps and Subarus to hike through the woods. Private property signs didn't hinder a few of them.

Then those damned archaeologists arrived from Florida State. Some kid found a piece of pottery and these academic types came down to dig up an old Indian site.

For the next six months, Gray skulked around, trying to run the archaeologists off. Of course, everything he did was behind the scenes. He imported some desperate meth addicts from Tampa and Tallahassee who gladly stole every piece of valuable equipment they could get their hands on. When the school countered with a security guard at night, he had the first security guard killed on Highway 98 in what looked like a single car accident. The second guard vanished from the job along with several laptops and other surveying equipment. The third was killed on sight by the jealous ex-boyfriend of the girl he'd started seeing since moving here—he was found at his trailer with the knife and plenty of DNA. It only took an anonymous phone call.

Still, the archaeologists weren't going away.

After that, the school scaled back their work, but they didn't go away. Contractors came in with chainlink fencing to cordon off the dig. Gray now worried that too much pressure would bring in authorities he didn't want snooping through the woods. For now, the archaeologists were safe, even if they weren't treated cordially by the locals.

Then the girl showed up looking for some pirate hideout or something. All Gray saw was another influx of archaeologists trying to dig up the past in his backyard.

That had to be stopped.

But now, someone came looking for her, and his eldest son likely drowned because of it.

He dreaded the next few minutes, but he'd put them off too long already. He rose from his seat in his office just off the kitchen in his modest home nestled back off a dirt road. When he stepped out of his sanctuary, his eyes rested on his wife, preparing something in the kitchen.

He swallowed as he prepared to tell her the news.

7

My back pressed against a tree, and I leaned my head against the bark. The mud caked in my hair hardened in the heat. Normally, my standard boat attire was a tank top, shorts or swimsuit, and sandals. I opted for a different look. After all, common sense suggested I protect myself from the incessant mosquitoes in these woods. So before I left, I donned jeans and hiking boots. Now thick, heavy coats of brown Florida swamp muck layered both. It was an especially pungent type, which soured a little more with the sun. However, the layers of mire drying on my arm deterred the insects. Or, at least, armored me against their bites.

I needed a plan. When I ventured up the river, I half-expected to putter around finding nothing. Instead, I ran head-to-head with trouble. It seemed reasonable to assume Rikki did the same thing.

Machete brightened at the idea of a reward, and if they had killed and dropped Rikki at the bottom of the river, it was unlikely he'd have that reaction. Plus, he mentioned getting Dexter's number directly from Rikki. At the very least, he didn't kill her.

What to do with that? Machete had settled into the silty riverbed, so he would not divulge any answers.

I could walk back to the coast. It might be a fifteen-mile hike, which was easy enough even in the wooded terrain. If I left now, I should make it before dark, but just barely.

However, Rikki wasn't in that direction.

Machete and, who I guessed was, his brother rode down the waterway on the WaveRunners. They were somewhere upriver then. If Machete couldn't help me, then Pistol Boy would have to do. Or the old man who clocked me with the butt of the shotgun.

In fact, I felt like I owed him for that.

I would need to find fresh water at some point. The river was one source, but I'd prefer to filter or boil it before I started sipping up the bacteria swimming in those waters.

With the faintest outline of a plan, I hiked along the river's edge. Or rather, on the rise of earth running along the river. The tree line started there, and it would provide cover if anyone approached on the water again. It also kept me up off the actual shore, where I had a better chance of stumbling across the Florida wildlife that might be bigger than the little fellow I'd seen earlier. Of course, alligators can climb hills, so the higher ground wouldn't be a hundred percent safe. But I like the odds of seeing the beasts up here.

After a quarter of a mile, I picked up a couple of intact and fairly fresh beer cans—one Coors Light and one Natural Light. I continued along until I found a plastic Coca-Cola bottle with a top attached. The red label still shone brightly, indicating it hadn't been in the sun long enough to bleach it. When I located a wide path to the water's edge, where I was fairly certain I was alone, I rinsed all three containers before filling the Coke bottle with water.

While it didn't look as crystal clear as a bottle of Evian from the cooler at the 7-Eleven, it was still clean water. At least to the eye.

I hiked back into the woods and gathered up some twigs and branches. Outdoor survival was one of the many things the service taught me. While I went through countless courses on surviving in the desert, I picked up a few tricks applicable everywhere.

Number one on the list of survival was almost always water. It might fall directly under "don't get killed by something with teeth" but it was certainly high on the agenda. Dehydration killed more people in the wild than bears or alligators. In Afghanistan, I drank three gallons a day just to keep up with how much I sweated out. Of course, if I didn't stop by 1800 hours, I'd pee all night. It was a delicate balance.

Once I gathered enough tinder, it took a few minutes to get a fire started. While the flames ate up the kindling, I ripped the tops of both cans off with the blade.

The plan was for me to fill the makeshift pots with the somewhat clean river water, and I would nestle the cans in the coals until they boiled. There was an inherent issue with heating beer cans. Almost all domestic brewers coated the inside of the can with BPA. A quick search of the internet left many fearful of drinking out of even a water bottle. However, as someone smarter than me explained—and I could only assume it was correct—the level of toxicity was fairly minimal. But I doubted I'd go through this trouble if I found a water fountain.

I settled onto the ground, leaning against a tree as I waited. Once I boiled two cans of water, I'd let them cool before filling the plastic bottle. Ideally, I'd start two more boiling, so I had plenty of fluids. But I didn't want to wait around for the water in my bottle to cool enough to drink it.

After serving in the desert, one of my least favorite things in the world was hot water. Inevitably, I'd drink all but the last two inches when some task pulled me away. In ten minutes, the rest at the bottom continued to heat. Without fail, I'd take a swallow, only to spew it out because the scalding water surprised me.

No, once it was in the Coke bottle, I'd let it cool as I made tracks along the river.

It took fifteen minutes for the water to bubble, and I boiled it for a full two minutes before moving the cans away from the coals. I had removed my shirt, letting the heat from the flames dry it. Now, I used it as an oven mitt, saving my fingers from a severe scalding. It needed to cool enough to be poured safely into the bottle without melting the sides.

I'd climbed out of the river nearly three hours ago, and now I was feeling the thirst come over me. Luckily, under the canopy of the trees, I wasn't as hot as out in the sun. Of course, this was still Florida where it was often ninety-eight degrees in the shade. Plus, there was the humidity—a beast in itself.

The smart move would have been to head back to *Carina* and *Talitha* to regroup. But Machete was already scheming how to turn Rikki over for a reward from her father—that meant he might know she was alive. Given the gleam in his eyes, I was certain he knew she was alive.

Or at least he did.

I doubted he had her prisoner somewhere, though. Rikki was smart enough to offer a reward on her own, even if she never mentioned her father.

No—Machete knew she was alive, but not where she was. At least, not exactly where she was.

That gave me more hope than I started with yesterday when I set out from *Talitha*. Rikki might still be alive.

Now, where was she?

The metal cans still radiated heat, but I touched them without blistering my fingers. I gently squeezed the round opening to create a spout before pouring the clean, if not purified, water into the bottle. The two cans filled it completely, leaving about two inches in the second can.

I cringed, but drained the remainder of the hot liquid into my mouth.

Think of it as really weak coffee, Gordon.

Even hot water would help quench my thirst, and if I knew it was going to be hot, it didn't seem as bad.

Through the trees, I heard the rumble of a motor. It didn't sound like a boat or WaveRunner. Plus, the noise traveled from the opposite direction of the river. An ATV of some sort. The high-pitched whine signaled the drivers were racing with the throttle wide open. I stomped out the fire and dropped into a running crouch.

As I scurried through the underbrush, I scanned the surrounding forest. Old growth filled the dense woods. This stretch of the coast avoided most of the hurricanes. That meant the vegetation didn't get mowed over every couple of years. It also meant either the ATV driver knew the woods well enough to race through the trees or there was a trail.

The other thought that crept into my head suggested that the driver's high speed could be because they were looking for me.

The smoke.

It was a gamble, and I even considered it for a few seconds before I started the fire. I felt the reward was worth the risk—a stupid assumption. I'd just killed Machete, and his friends would want to do something about that. Even if they were only coming back to retrieve his body, the smoke might signal them to make a direct beeline to it.

I rolled under a thicket of blackberry bushes entwined in a jumble. The thorns ripped across my bare shoulders, and I cursed myself for not putting my shirt on before I took cover.

From my hiding hole, I peered out and waited.

In just shy of two minutes, a Polaris RZR came into view with a couple of men strapped side by side. The driver slowed as they began searching the woods.

There were some shouts over the engine, but I couldn't make out what they said. Neither of the two men were the ones I encountered earlier. Both were far younger than the graying man, and neither one was the guy with the twenty-two.

However, both carried two 30-06 rifles with scopes strung over their torsos. It seemed unlikely they were hunting on a $40,000 trailblazer like that.

At least, they weren't hunting wildlife.

The passenger pointed toward the river—in the direction of my fire. I didn't see any smoke from here, but that meant little. The breeze could carry the smell easily toward them.

I strained my neck slowly to see behind them. They weren't on a trail at the moment, but they'd slowed down too. Probably there was a path leading them most of the way here. That also meant it led most of the way out. Hopefully, I could follow it to where they came from.

Not that it would do me any good. If Rikki was alive and hiding out in the woods, I didn't think she'd head toward these guys. She was too smart for that.

She was also savvy enough to know better than to stray too far away from all civilization. And why wouldn't she just make for the coast? That made the most sense.

Unless she was injured.

Or something kept her from going that direction.

Or she was just damned stubborn.

Right now, I hoped for the third option. Although, if I found her hurt, I might have an easier time hauling her out over my shoulder than if she'd dug in her heels.

The Polaris bounced over a log as it rocked back and forth through the trees. Then the engine died.

"There it is," the passenger stated. His voice was now clear, without the overbearing rumble of the Polaris.

He climbed out of the off-road vehicle. The rifle in his hand raised up, and he peered down the scope as he swept it slowly around.

"See anything?" the driver, a dirty-looking blond man in his thirties, asked. The accent was pure rural Florida—something altogether different from the rest of the South.

"Not yet," the passenger replied. He continued searching the area where I'd been. "Wait."

The passenger bounded off the Polaris and moved through the brush toward the remnants of my fire.

"What is it?"

The man pointed at the smoldering coals. "A fire."

The driver climbed out of the vehicle, raised his 30-06, and followed along. "Think it's Jace?"

The passenger knelt by the ashes.

"Hopper?" the driver asked.

"It's fresh. Ten minutes ago, maybe," Hopper answered.

"Jace!" the driver shouted.

"Wait," Hopper interjected in a hushed reprimand. "I don't think this is Jace."

The driver lifted his rifle up, spinning around anxiously. "What makes you say that?"

"If it was Jace, he'd have heard us coming. He would be trying to wave us down," Hopper explained. "This fire was kicked out quickly."

He lifted one of the beer cans up to show the driver. "He was boiling water."

The driver didn't take his right eye off the scope as he acknowledged Hopper. "I don't see anyone," he reported. "He could be gone."

Hopper straightened up. He stared through the trees in my direction. I didn't think he saw me, but I tightened my grip on the machete. If they got close enough, I could defend myself. However, at this distance, the rifles, in the hands of someone who could use them, would drop me with one shot. It hardly mattered where they hit me, either. The 30-06 round made a nice clean hole when it entered the body, but the exit wound looked like something from a horror movie burst out of the skin.

Don't breathe.

"He went that way," Hopper announced, pointing right along the path I'd taken.

Either Hopper noticed something obvious, like a footprint in the mud, or he was some wunderkind redneck in the backwoods of Florida that knew how to track a field mouse. I hoped it was the former. The tangle of blackberry bushes obscured me for now, but if they got closer, it was game over. If the dirty blond guy actually knew how to follow tracks, he'd walk right to me.

I'd seen guys who were trackers. Somehow, they saw something different in the landscape. A broken twig. Bent grass. Things that looked like regular background to the rest of us.

These two moved toward me slowly. They were natural hunters—probably stalking deer since they were old enough to hold a rifle. Despite their blaring entrance on the Polaris, the two now fell into a silence as they stalked my direction.

I calculated how I could disarm either of them, hoping if I was fast enough, the other would hesitate shooting if I held his friend hostage. From my position, it was a difficult move. I'd need to spring up through the brambles on them before they got a shot off. None of the scenarios I played out in my head ended well. Hopper and the driver were just far enough apart to make it impossible to neutralize both, meaning the other would have ample opportunity to turn and fire.

The two men took meticulous steps, making no sound as they moved like foxes tiptoeing through the leaves. If I hadn't watched them from the start, I wouldn't hear them coming. It was a technique similar to some of the training in the Corps. One officer referred to it as "fox-stepping" where the foot gently comes down on one side and rolled against the ground until the heel touched. It was rigorous and slow, but over time, the action became rote. These two mastered the movement.

They were dangerous. Real hunters usually were. I imagined Hopper and his friend bagged their limits every season. What worried me more was the blackness in their eyes. I didn't think I was the first person they ever hunted, either. It was too easy to drop into the predator mode for them. Most people couldn't slip into the killer mindset unless it, too, had become familiar.

Nothing about the two men indicated they had any formal training. Neither moved like they had military instruction. This didn't make them less dangerous. It just gave me a brief insight into them.

When they were less than twenty feet from me, they paused. My eyes closed for a second, preparing to jump at them.

Behind them, the Polaris roared to life. Both men swiveled their heads as the RZR bolted away.

"Shit!" Hopper shouted. "He doubled back."

The two spun around, running toward the fleeing vehicle.

8

"Shit!" Hopper shouted, turning away from me.

I didn't move. While I held my breath, every muscle tightened in preparation for whatever might come next.

"He doubled back," the other one cried. "Dammit, Hopper!"

Leaves rustled as both men ran in the opposite direction. A few seconds later, I heard gunshots. They were firing away from me—at someone else. Wasting no time, I rolled to my feet and dragged myself through the blackberry bush. The thicket caught in my clothing like barbed wire, scratching at my face and arms. The sticky air blew over the fresh slices with a burning sensation.

More gunfire.

I peered through the brambles and spotted Hopper aiming his rifle at the fleeing Polaris. The ATV roared away, cutting off the trail and through the trees.

He squinted through the scope and muttered an expletive. "It's that girl!

Shoot her," the other one encouraged, slapping Hopper on the shoulder.

My stomach clenched—could it be Rikki?

The gun cracked, but Hopper had missed her. There was no time to help Rikki or whoever was escaping on their ATV. I scrambled away, desperately trying to remain silent despite my racing heart. Once I had put some distance between me and my hiding spot, I crouched behind a cypress tree, watching in horror as Hopper slowly turned back to where I had been moments earlier.

His partner paused, staring at the smoldering ash on the ground, and asked, "Did she start the fire?"

While Hopper rotated to look where I'd been standing seconds ago, my mind raced for an escape route. Staying low, I made it to a large cypress tree some fifty feet away.

"Eric," Hopper hissed.

He wasn't in my line of sight, but I imagined he directed him to split off. As I listened to the footsteps, I confirmed the two were splitting away from each other. Maybe Hopper couldn't get a good read on my trail since I tried to step a little more carefully. Whatever it was, I counted it as a blessing.

Of course, I was still unarmed with nowhere to run. I pressed my back against the tree and waited. If only one came my direction, I hoped I could surprise him. I really prayed the other didn't shoot me while I was grappling with his friend. Most people wouldn't, but I'd encountered a few with ice-cold blood pumping through their heart.

My breaths grew shallow as every sound seemed amplified in the eerie silence of the trees. The crack of a stick echoed like thunder in my ears and I knew he had stopped right on the spot, waiting to see if anyone else had heard it. Ten seconds seemed an eternity until he stepped again, each footstep ringing out a death march coming ever closer toward me.

There was rarely any movement, no matter how slow or slight, through the woods that can be completely silent. Even squirrels and birds often make a raucous noise. Especially when the rest of the forest remained still.

Right now, a deathly silence hung heavy in the air amongst the trees, which only caused every single motion he made seem to echo off the trunks. The trees themselves were pointing back at him. He cautiously crept toward the cypress, trying, unsuccessfully, not to make a sound.

Suddenly I saw it—the barrel of his gun slowly appearing around the corner of the trunk. But I was ready. My right hand shot out and caught it before he could fire off a round. In one swift motion, I yanked down on the 30-06 and drove the butt into his face with bone-shattering force.

He grunted as the butt slammed into his mouth. Again and again, I shoved the stock of the rifle into him until Eric released his grip. As if driven by a will of its own, my left wrist rotated and caught hold of the gun, curling around it tightly and snuggling my fingers into the trigger guard.

Across the woods, Hopper whipped in a semicircle and raised his own 30-06 my direction—but not before I squeezed the trigger. When the round exited the barrel, it shot out at roughly 2400 feet per second and punctured through Hopper's chest before the echo of the explosion resounded among the trees. The impact lifted him off the ground by a few inches and threw him back into the blackberry bush where I'd been hiding only a few minutes earlier. A branch cracked from the force of his body and he collapsed to the earth with an audible thud.

Eric exploded forward with a roar and hit me like a linebacker. He was faster than I expected and drove his shoulder into me, just above my belt. The attack knocked the breath out of my lungs as I dropped back, hitting the dirt with a thump. His bloodied face was twisted in an uncontrollable rage and he scrambled up my chest, throwing punches at my head. I lifted the 30-06 rifle between us and used it as a shield to block his blows, but could only deflect half of them. He tried to wrestle it away from me, pushing down hard on the stock while his right fist moved rapidly between my eyes. All I could do was try to hold him off.

My body jerked in an undulating motion, trying to throw him off me, but he held on tight. With all my might, I flung my feet in the air, and as they came down, I thrust my pelvis up and pivoted.

The move knocked him off balance, and I rolled to the side, sending him flailing to the dirt. His legs thrashed wildly, and I scrambled back. His grasp on the 30-06 remained unbreakable, and we each pulled against the other as we both worked our way halfway to a kneeling position.

With a fierce tug, Eric gave the rifle another jerk. I let the tension out of my arms without losing my grip on the rifle. My sudden release unbalanced Eric, and before he regained his stance, I wrenched the weapon to me.

A deafening boom echoed in my ears as I pulled the trigger without hesitation. The force of the bullet ripped through his clavicle like tissue paper, sending him sprawling to the ground in a shower of bone and blood. He gasped for breath as he lay face down on the forest floor, his shattered remains resembling a bloody piece of raw beef.

Eric writhed in the dirt and leaves, reminding me of a snake in its own death throes. I took a giant step back with the butt of the 30-06 nestled against my shoulder. With two broad side steps, I rotated around 360 degrees. The woods were quieter after the gunshots as the wildlife either fled the scene or hunkered in place. Eric's muffled moans were the only noise.

"You'll live," I told the man, who barely seem to know I was still there. The gunshot wound shouldn't kill him unless I got lucky and hit a major artery. However, I was fairly certain that was not the case. It would, however, hurt like all hell rained down on him. The 30-06 round likely shattered his shoulder. After several seconds of wallowing face-first against the forest floor, Eric succumbed to the pain and blacked out.

I knelt over him, checking his breathing. It was heavy but not labored. I rolled him onto his back before dragging him to the cypress trunk. When I straightened up, the man appeared to be resting against the thick tree. His head lolled to the side as if he was sleeping. At least this way, he wouldn't suffocate in the dirt. That was probably more than he'd planned to do for me.

Once I propped him up, I went through his pockets. He had some loose rifle rounds, and I pulled them out, counting out ten bullets. He also had a small refillable water bottle in a holster on his belt. For a split second, I considered taking it, but decided not to take it from him. I'm the compassionate sort. Not so compassionate as to leave the hunting knife he had on the other side of his waist.

I moved over to Hopper's body. He carried a water bottle almost identical to Eric's. Hopper had no use for it anymore, and I didn't balk at relieving him of it. In his pockets, I found a small bundle of twelve bullets, $260 in cash, and an oat and honey-flavored granola bar. I took them all—spoils of war.

Before I left the body, I removed all the shells from Hopper's 30-06. I didn't want to lug two rifles with me, but there were two things I wanted to ensure: one, as much ammunition as I could carry. As a general rule, it was better to tote extra rounds than get myself in a situation where I didn't have enough. And two, I preferred not to leave bullets around that could find their way into my body. With that in mind, I carried the rifle away from the bodies before flinging it off the ridge toward the thicket of grass on the riverbank.

If Rikki stole the ATV, I wanted to start after her. The last time I saw the vehicle, it was heading west. I found the trail Hopper and Eric came down, and I followed along off to the side. No point in being too visible if some friends of those two showed up.

After tearing the granola bar wrapper, I pulled out one of the crunchy bars. With the first bite, I felt my hunger dissipate. The effect was mostly psychological, but that didn't stop it from being effective. The human body could function for a long while without sustenance, but the mind had a tendency to get in the way. It would not fill me up, but it would keep my brain thinking it was enough to go on.

In the distance, I heard the whine of an engine coming closer. The sound came from the west, and I quickly took cover behind another large tree. With the barrel of the 30-06 pointed upward and against my chest, I waited, ready to pop out and take aim in less than a second.

The noise drew nearer, and my head peeped around the trunk. Coming down the path was at least what looked like the same Polaris. From where I hid, I had a clear view. The vehicle was coming fast, and when it was about a hundred yards away, I raised the scope for a better look.

A slender African-American woman sat behind the wheel. Rikki appeared far more weathered than the last time I was with her, but several days in these humid woods might weather anyone. I lifted the rifle and stepped into the path, leaving myself enough room to dodge her if she chose to run over me. After all, I doubted she expected to see me stomping through the leaves.

She braked in the path when she saw me. The Polaris came to a stop nearly a hundred feet from me. A steady rumble came from the engine, and she stared at me for a full seven seconds before she eased the vehicle forward.

When she came up beside me, she studied me without a word for several seconds.

"What the hell are you doing here?" she finally asked.

"I thought a nice romantic cruise up the river would be fun," I told her with a smile.

"The fucking rednecks are an added bonus?"

I shrugged, still holding my grin. A roar echoed through the trees, and I turned my head to the east, where two white ATVs zoomed down the path toward us.

"Get in," she ordered. "Before I leave you here."

My hand grabbed the roll cage over the seats and swung into the passenger seat. Rikki gunned the engine before I settled into the chair.

9

I barely fit the seat belt around me when Rikki cut the wheel to the left and floored the accelerator. Inertia threw me to the right, and I was glad I got the buckle fastened. The back of the Polaris fishtailed slightly as she regained the traction she needed.

Over my shoulder, I checked to see the other two ATVs. Both were white, and from where I was sitting looked almost identical to this one. They probably weren't exact, but once a manufacturer found a nice mold, they wanted to duplicate it over and over.

The styles and makes of the vehicles didn't matter. The fact that they were coming up fast on our ass worried me. From what I'd encountered so far this morning, these guys didn't mind exerting deadly force.

"Who are these guys, anyway?" I asked, gripping the bar on the dash in front of me as the tires bounced over a log.

"Hell if I know," Rikki shouted over the din of the racing engine. "They are everywhere I turn."

"Hang on!" she added.

"I've been hanging on!" I exclaimed. My right hand released the bar and grabbed the strap above my head. Those handholds were on most cars, and where I grew up in Arkansas, we affectionately called them the "Oh Shit Bars."

"Oh, shit!" I yelped as Rikki cut the wheel to jump off the path. The rear tire of the ATV bounced off the trunk of an oak tree, and like a pinball, the entire vehicle changed direction. Rikki fought the ATV to bring it back under control as she weaved through the trees.

Our pursuers followed us into the trees with less incident, gaining them a few feet.

"I hope you know what you're doing," I shouted.

"You want to drive?" she questioned as she spun the ATV to the left, causing me to slide across the seat toward her.

I didn't hear the first gunshot. Instead, the ping as it ricocheted off the metal frame was all I heard.

"They're shooting at us," Rikki pointed out.

"I'm unbuckling," I warned her. "Don't throw me out."

"No promises," she responded, her eyes locked ahead as she maneuvered through the trees.

The belt snapped back when I released it. The 30-06 lifted over the seat as I twisted around.

I was usually a pretty good shot, but I doubted my aim could match Jay Delp's. Jay, my best friend served with me in the Corps, had eyes like a hawk and never missed anything he aimed for, making him the deadliest sniper I knew. He took first place two years in a row at the Marine Scout Sniper Challenge. Of course, his training went beyond friendly games.

But right now, with the ATV zig-zagging through these tricky ridges and bumps, I didn't think I'd have much of a chance at hitting our pursuers. Still, I hoped I could at least slow them down.

Through the rifle's scope, I strained to focus on the forward ATV as it continued to zip in and out of view as Rikki whipped left or right. After a few seconds, I could almost feel the rhythm of the motion in my hands, and when, for a split second, the driver's head passed through the crosshairs, I pulled the trigger with a satisfying click. The bullet flew just past him, grazing his shoulder and causing him to swerve violently away from its trajectory. His left tire crashed into a nearby tree with a deafening thud, bringing the vehicle screeching to an abrupt halt.

The second ATV dropped back a bit as it weaved through the trees, leaving me without a single shot.

"Grab something!" Rikki shouted at me.

I released the 30-06's stock with my left hand and grabbed the steel tubing over our heads just as the Polaris came off the ground. I didn't see what Rikki jumped. From my perspective, I saw the rear tires fly above the earth as inertia flung me out of my seat and through the opening on the right. My other hand dropped the rifle, grabbing for anything as I flapped out the rear like a flag.

The wheels landed with a bounce, and I fell into the seat and rolled onto the floor. My hand reached up and grabbed the dash, pulling me back up into my seat.

"Did I lose the gun?" I half-asked as I stretched the belt across me, still dazed.

Rikki cut her eyes to me and offered, "Sorry. I can go back."

When I turned back, I saw the drop we'd made. Rikki took us off a twenty-foot ridge into what I guessed was an old riverbed. At the top of the ridge, the other white ATV sat. The driver stood up in his seat, taking a quick survey of the route. They hadn't moved by the time we took the next curve and lost sight of them.

Rotating back around, I let out a sigh. "No, I don't think I need it." I congratulated her. "Nice job. That's some fancy driving you're doing."

"It won't take them long to go around and find a better way down," she advised. "We need to get far away from here."

"Yeah, and this thing makes enough noise. They can follow us for miles."

Rikki climbed the other dry bank into the trees.

"Wait," I urged her, and she stopped.

I jumped off the ATV and ran back to the dry riverbed. The tires compressed the grass where Rikki drove out of the gulch. My feet brushed the grass back, trying to get it to stand up again. It was far from perfect, but hopefully it wasn't as obvious as it had been at first. Anything that could divert their attention would give us some extra time.

I ran back and climbed into the Polaris. "Go!" I ordered, and Rikki drove on without opening the throttle all the way.

We drove a mile into the woods, where we found a thicket. The tall oak trunks stood like columns in a cathedral, so close together that only enough light could filter through for small plants to grow and for birds to fly between them. Rikki backed the ATV into the brush, and I climbed out and helped her tie back the vines and branches so that they encircled the machine like a sheath. Much like the grass, it was far from obscured, but it might not draw immediate attention.

"Come on," Rikki told me. "We can head this way."

"Where are we going?"

"There's an old campground," she explained. "It looks like it used to be a state-run thing, but it's overgrown now. They must have forgotten about it at least twenty years ago."

"Have you had any water?" I asked her.

She turned to look at me with incredulous eyes. "Do I look like I'm dehydrated to you?"

"Geez, I don't remember you being this quick to bite my head off," I remarked.

Rikki crossed her arms and glared at me. "What are you doing here?"

"I—"

"No, let me guess," she spouted. "Sam called you."

"He's worried about you."

"Come on," she repeated. I stepped in line with her.

"What happened Rikki?"

"Let's talk about it later," she suggested. "These are the busiest damned woods you'll ever see."

"How many are out there?"

She shrugged as she walked. "I didn't count, but enough I can't go in any direction without running into several of them."

I said nothing. Rikki was right. If someone was following the sound of the ATV, they might get close. Our voices might reach out through the woods. The less we talked, the more difficult it would be to pinpoint where we were.

Rikki had had few days to learn the terrain, and she marched like she knew exactly where she needed to end up. Our heading took us on a slightly northwest path. At some point, the trees began closing in on us, and the Spanish moss loomed over us as if it wanted to scoop us into the canopy.

My stomach was grumbling again. The one granola bar hadn't fended off the hunger, and the adrenaline rush of the chase through the woods didn't help. Once we got settled, I could figure out some food.

Rikki was taking us farther from the river, and I wondered if she'd eaten much lately. She didn't appear malnourished. After the reaction I got about the water, I held my tongue a bit longer. Maybe she found a stash of MREs buried out here.

Something to the right crashed through the woods, and I froze, scanning the trees until I caught sight of the flickering white tail of a deer escaping whatever danger it thought we posed. Since I lost the rifle, it only had to fear the hunting knife I took off Eric. It's not that I couldn't kill a deer with just a knife, but it was a much more laborious task.

When I turned back, I found Rikki had vanished. Several small evergreens grew together in a small copse, and I pushed through them. On the other side, the forest widened. The old-growth trees hung back, and at first, I mistook the area for a small meadow until I noticed the odd shapes rising out of the grass. Picnic tables. Old concrete ones that had endured the weather. Years chipped off several of the corners. Rusted rebar metal jutted out from the jagged edges.

Rikki waded through thigh-high tall grass about thirty feet ahead of me. I followed along, studying the surrounding field. The dilapidated remnants of a covered picnic area stood across the way. Its roof sported holes throughout, and it long ceased offering any protection from the weather.

I watched Rikki climb up onto a picnic table. When I reached her, I noticed the area under the table had been cleared away.

"You've been sleeping here?" I asked.

"It's somewhat protected, and the grass practically hides the table completely."

I couldn't disagree, and I climbed up next to her.

"Sorry I snapped earlier," she apologized.

"I was a little glib," I replied.

"That's kind of your go-to, though," she pointed out.

"I am what I am," I said.

"One would think a big bad Marine wouldn't quote a Navy man," she joked with a grin.

My arm wrapped around her and pulled her next to me. "It's been too long," I told her.

10

Rikki leaned her head against my shoulder, trembling. She let out a long, exhausted sigh.

"How did you evade them?" I asked, my voice strained. "These guys tried to kill me three times this morning alone."

"Mostly, I stayed holed up here ever since they arrived," she replied. "A few guys came past, but none of them looked closely enough. One even walked right by without noticing me cowering under the table. He was too busy bitching about having to find me. Most of them don't strike me as the smartest wolves in the pack. I'm not sure what they are hiding, or who is in charge, but so far, most of these guys operate on brute force."

"Don't knock brute force," I remarked. "They almost ran us down that way."

"It might have been easier for me just to hide," she commented. "It's a big forest for them to search."

"Why didn't you make a run to the coast?" I asked.

"It's impossible, there's too many of those rednecks guarding the buildings and barriers," Rikki answered hopelessly. "I tried getting through once at night, but they were more alert than usual. They were moving crates around like their lives depended on it."

"What happened to you?" I urged her to continue. "Honestly, I didn't think I'd find you after so long."

"What did Sam tell you?"

"It was Milo who reached out first." I paused, remembering the worry they had about Rikki's safety. "He came looking for me down in the Keys."

"Really?" she asked with some awe.

"Yeah, he and Sam were worried sick about you."

"So why did you come?" She stared up at me.

I shrugged. "Why wouldn't I?"

"We haven't talked in a year," she pointed out. "Not even a phone call or email."

"It's about time we caught up, right?" I suggested. "Besides, you know I don't have a phone and email has never been my thing."

"Stop it, Chase. It's insane."

"Don't worry, I'm always going to be your cavalry."

Her face lit up with a smile. "I'd do the same for you too," she assured me.

"That's what I'm counting on," I replied. Then, lightheartedly changing the topic, I said, "What have you been up to lately?"

"Oh, just doing a new workout regimen of running away from rednecks and eating nothing but nuts and acorns," she answered. "It's done wonders for my core."

I leaned back on the bench and gave her an impressed look before saying, "It looks good on you—though you should consider taking a shower, too."

Rikki chuckled at that. "Coming from someone whose ears are caked in mud, that means a lot!"

Automatically, I wiped my hand against my earlobe and knocked off a chunk of brown goo. "Ah, this is all part of the spa package I signed up for," I joked. "Comes with a complimentary mud bath."

"This place is all-inclusive."

"Milo said you were on the trail for Gasparilla," I commented.

"A very thin lead," she explained. "I hoped to meet with an archaeologist doing a dig up here."

"But..."

"The site was east of here. There was a town on the river called Clay's Landing. Mostly it was a riverboat stop, but if Gasparilla made his way up the Suwannee River, it was a sure bet he'd put in there."

"What were you looking for?"

"At this point, anything. It is probably just a wild goose chase," she explained. "Gasparilla has so little written history. Instead, he's the stuff of legend. Stories tell that he buried his wife and treasure together. But that's all it is. Just stories."

"I didn't think you chased after things without some evidence," I pointed out.

"Not usually," she answered. "It was stupid. I've been bored lately. Every potential hunt has fizzled out."

"So, you wanted to do something?"

She nodded. "Do I know when to pick a dumb quest or what? Run off into the only woods guarded by Klan rejects."

"If you are lucky, these hicks are hiding a hillbilly treasure."

"Of what?" she questioned. "Meth?"

"It would be worth a fortune," I advised.

"I'm already worth a fortune," she reminded me.

It occurred to me that despite joking about it, that might be exactly what was going on here. This many men patrolling a forest, not to mention that Rikki saw them moving freight of some kind. If they were running methamphetamines through these woods, that would be ample reason to kill over it.

"What did they do to you?" I asked.

"When I found the dig or, at least, what was left of it, two police officers showed up. I thought they were going to give me trouble for trespassing, and I shot Sam a message. They must not have known that, or I think they'd have kept up the pretense. Instead, they tried to get a little handsy with me. I realized I would not make it out of the woods alive if I went with them."

"What did you do?"

"Played along," she explained. "When the first opportunity presented itself, I took off. Made it into the water. I was sure they'd catch up to me or something would. I stayed under as long as I could before I popped back up. After that, I allowed the current to carry me a bit before I got out."

"Why not let it take you all the way to the Gulf?"

Rikki shook her head. "Nope, when I saw the ten-foot gator slide into the water, I hightailed it to the other shore. I can handle what's in the woods, but those bastards don't surface before they drag you under."

"Afraid of a little lizard?" I asked.

"Hell, no. But I'm wise enough to stay out of their way."

"What's to the east, then?" I asked.

"More of them. It's like everyone is related too. Or maybe they all just live here."

"If I remember my geography, we don't have any towns to the east, anyway. Possibly a couple of little hamlets."

Rikki shook her head. "There's Como. About five miles from here—on the edge of the state forest."

"That's probably who the cops worked for," I pointed out.

"It did say it on their uniforms," she acknowledged.

"Guess our best bet is west, then. I think we're still fifteen or so miles from the coast. We just need to get past your goon squad."

She nodded.

"What are they guarding, anyway?" I asked.

"About six Quonset huts. They have it surrounded by a chain-link fence, complete with razor wire. From what I could see, the fence runs all the way to the river. Or, at least, pretty damned close to it."

"Hmm," I mused.

"You're thinking they are smuggling drugs out of here, right?"

I smiled. "You already considered the same thing."

"It makes sense," she stated. "The most tourism they get around here is eco-friendly. Fisherman, mostly, I'd guess. Somehow, they keep them away from their operation."

"Easy enough. Keep the boaters on the water," I said. "Look what happened when we stepped on land. They don't want anyone staying around too long."

"Surely they can't kill everyone that comes upstream?" she questioned.

"No, it's easier to run off the few that stick around too long. I even heard them early this morning. They weren't going to do anything if I left on my own. Since I didn't, they stepped in."

"That's a big escalation to jump from doing nothing to killing you."

I nodded. "That might have been my fault. I asked about you, and they got a bit more aggressive."

"You did everything you could to deescalate that situation, I'm sure."

"If there's one thing you can say about me, it's that I try to only choose violence as a last resort."

Rikki gave a small chuckle. "Did you this time?"

"Actually, I did. Mostly because they knocked me out. Their plan was to drop me in the middle of the river."

"That sounds like what they wanted to do to me too," Rikki noted. "Although they might have had additional intentions with me."

I released a deep sigh. There wasn't much to say to that. The longer I was around people, the less I like them.

"We need to get out of here," I told her.

"Those bastards took my gear," Rikki remarked.

"What kind of stuff?"

"Everything I had. My notes, knife, and maps."

"Maps to what?" I asked.

She shrugged. "A few old ones I got from Milo."

"He will be upset when they don't come back."

"We could go get them," she offered.

"You didn't even want to sneak past the guards, and now you think we should walk in and ask for your bag of maps?"

Rikki's teeth gleamed as she flashed me a smile. "You ever have a little dog that gets all ferocious when it's backed up by a big Doberman?"

"Somehow I think you actually know you are the Doberman."

"How many men have you killed today?" she asked.

"Let's not play that game then," I scolded her. Something people often did was make light of the actions people like me did. Anytime I took a life, it was deserved. That didn't make me feel good about it, and while I might try to keep those ominous thoughts cordoned off with macabre humor, it wasn't someone else's place to joke about it.

"No maps, huh?" she questioned.

I shook my head. "Milo will be much happier if you are safe than that his maps are back."

"It irritates me," she moaned.

With a nod, I agreed. Rikki was formidable, but this was pure bravado. She'd been more afraid than I realized. Fear was an emotion she didn't seem to feel a great deal. Last year, when we were trapped underground together, she remained solid and stoic. This time, she felt much closer to whatever end result those cops intended for her than she was used to. Rikki maintained control all the time, and somehow they took that. Now she wanted it back.

Unfortunately, her plan to wrest it away was neither viable nor advisable.

"We have a couple of hours till it gets dark," I told her. "Let's rest up. We can scout it out after the sun goes down and see how to get through."

Rikki nodded, proceeding to climb under the table. "The shade makes it slightly cooler," she told me.

I followed her beneath the concrete slab. After some twisting and contorting, I squeezed my frame into the opening. I stretched out on my back, and Rikki sat up on her elbow staring at me.

"I know I'm a little gross, but can I rest on you?"

My brow furrowed. "Of course."

"I mean, we haven't talked in over a year," she said. "You might be married or celibate."

My left eyebrow arched. "Not likely."

"What about the lady at your hotel?"

"Missy? We are as much of a thing as one can be when she's got a husband."

The corners of her mouth turned up slightly as she leaned her head over and let it press against my chest. "Good. I was just tired of my head being on the concrete."

"I'm forever at your service."

"It doesn't have all the rough edges."

I laughed. "Some people probably disagree with you."

"Meh," she muttered, turning a bit to get more comfortable.

We lay there silently for a few minutes. The chirping and buzzing of bugs was the only sound.

"What about you?" I asked.

"Me?"

"Yeah. Are you married or celibate or anything?"

"Just anything, Chase."

"I'm not sure what that means."

"It is an implication that when we get back to the boat, I plan to ravage you."

My head lifted so I could gaze down on her still face. "Why wait?"

"You smell like a dung pile."

"So do you, and it wouldn't stop me," I pointed out.

"Yeah, that only shows that your standards are lower than mine."

"Hmph," I grunted.

The insects continued their screeching.

"Chase?" Rikki said. The bugs ignored her interruption.

"Yeah."

"Thanks for dropping whatever to come find me."

"What can I say?" I responded. "My standards are low."

She gave my chest a playful swat before falling back into silence.

11

Cicadas screamed into the darkness with a fury that filled the woods in every direction. If only the shrieks fended off the swarms of mosquitoes hovering around us. Florida had its fair share of undesirable creatures, from snakes to alligators. The worst, by far, were these tiny blood-sucking bastards. Unlike in some places, these little beasts never went dormant. Their only purpose in life was to breed, suck, grow, die. Unfortunately, they seemed to me to do the first three much better than the last. Each time they attacked during the day, I wondered if they ever rested. However, those were the skeleton crew because once the stars came out, so did most of the buzzing things.

The caked mud helped, and I wanted to take advantage of the camouflage aspects it offered. Rikki and I didn't have to walk all the way back to the river. The state constructed the former campground, where we took refuge next to a small creek that coursed eventually into the Suwannee. It was perfect for a supply of natural camo and bug repellent. Since I didn't want to give away our location with another fire, we skipped the pretense of boiling water, and we both drank from the stream. At least the stream flowed quickly—a good sign it wasn't stagnant and hopefully safer to consume.

Rikki led me to a raspberry bush on the bank of the creek. I gave her my other granola bar, assuming she might need it more than I did. The vines were heavy with berries, although, being the wild variety, the fruit was smaller and more tart than something cultivated. Still, they were delicious, and I felt better after eating several handfuls.

"You should stay here," I urged her. "Let me sneak in and take a look."

"It's too far," she reasoned. "If you find a way through, you'd have to double back to get me."

"That's still the safest plan," I advised.

"It's a stupid plan," she refuted. "I'm going with you."

I groaned. "Fine, but you are staying back while I scout ahead. Someplace safe, so I don't have to worry about you."

Even in the dark, the whites of her eyes were obvious as she rolled them. "You're sexist."

"That's not true," I argued. "Tactically, it makes sense for only one of us to approach at first. The United States government spent a lot of money training me for covert surveillance."

Rikki sneered at me. "I'm still going," she stubbornly insisted.

Futility was something I tried not to go up against. She would not back down, and I couldn't exactly force her to stay here. Her point was valid, too. If there was a way past, the wise course of action was to take advantage of it as quickly as possible. A return trip to the campground would add a couple of hours, at the very least. In that amount of time, we could cover half the distance to the Gulf.

That would put us in view of *Carina* and *Talitha* by daybreak. We could have breakfast on board, sandwiched between a long shower and a longer nap.

"Coat all your skin in mud," I told her. "It'll help hide you."

She stared at me, dumbfounded, before pointing out, "I'm black."

"Keeps the bugs off you too," I added.

She nodded with that realization before bending down to scoop up the thick, brown muck. I gathered the mud from the middle of the stream, trying to filter out the leaves and sticks. Most of what I had in my hands was smooth, comprised almost solely of dirt and water. My fingers rubbed the silt over my face, coating everything. My lips tasted earthy, and I spewed air from my mouth to blow the excess off them.

When I looked at Rikki, she returned the glance with a broad smile—her white teeth glowing through the muck.

"When we're done here, I think there's a place in Orlando where you can mud wrestle for a cash prize," I joked.

"It would be embarrassing to kick everyone's ass."

Once we were both sufficiently coated, I said, "Alright, let's get going."

"Lead the way, captain," she responded.

The hike took us nearly an hour and a half, but we walked an indirect route, cutting back and forth along the trail we'd been on earlier. Two four-wheelers rumbled, their bright LED headlights illuminating the forest for a hundred yards ahead of them. The sounds of the engines gave us ample time to slink behind some trees, hoping that if the lights hit us, the brown coating of mud would do its job and hide us.

"They looked like patrols," I commented after the ATVs were out of sight.

"Are they looking for us?" she asked.

"Not sure," I responded. They didn't operate like they were on a search. Each vehicle had two people on it. The driver remained focused on the trail ahead, and the passenger sat backward. I didn't have as good a line of sight on both, but at least one of the two sitting in the rear carried a rifle. In the dark, I couldn't distinguish the make either.

My gut said they were more of a deterrent. If no one had found us in the daylight, a nighttime search pushed the edges of fruitlessness. But I'd seen people do that regularly.

When we were closer to the buildings Rikki told me about, the artificial noise of civilization crept through the woods. A gentle whirring of an engine. Not a vehicle—the RPMs remained consistent. A generator was my guess.

After a minute, voices became clearer. Casual conversation, but the din of the motor garbled the words.

I paused, taking in the surrounding forest, at least what I could make out on this moonless night. The canopy above us drowned out the little light the stars might offer. But I made out the trunks of a few nearby trees.

"That tree there," I whispered to Rikki, pointing out an old-growth growing at an odd angle. "Get down there and wait for me."

"But—"

My right index finger shot up, stopping her next words. "I mean it. If I have to worry about you, this will take too long."

Her lips pursed in a pout. "Fine," she agreed reluctantly.

As she moved away, I crept in the direction of the hum and voices. As the noise grew louder, I realized I was closer than I thought. Whatever they did out of this compound, they determined to keep it under the radar. There were no exterior lights, and if the short arched buildings had power on the inside, I couldn't see it bleeding out from any windows.

With the construction, I expected to have at least some ambient light filter in where they thinned the trees to make room for the huts. When I glanced up, I realized why that wasn't occurring. They added a mesh across the top. It's a method used in the military too. Effective camouflage from the air. If they did it correctly, a satellite or airplane wouldn't see the break in the trees or the buildings in the clearing. Even a low-flying plane or chopper probably wouldn't notice. However, an experienced spotter might detect the difference.

An interesting, if not expensive, endeavor to keep this compound out of the prying eyes. I considered the structures, too. Quonset huts were designed for quick military use during the second world war. Someone could ship them anywhere to be thrown up quickly. This complex could have been developed in a week or two, perhaps less if pressed to do so.

Cigarette smoke drifted through the air, and I froze, turning my head slowly to see a man standing fifty feet away. The red glow of a cherry appeared, followed by the sound of a heavy exhale. My eyes took a second to adjust to the dark, but when they did, I felt a surge of panic. An outline on his forehead reminded me distinctly of night-vision glasses pulled up on his head.

He wasn't using them now—taking a smoke break. I lowered myself quietly to the earth and waited. The man finished his cigarette and flicked the stub into the woods. With a deep breath, he tugged the goggles down over his eyes and lifted a rifle up before walking softly forward.

At least one guy was outside the perimeter making rounds, and he had an advantage with the night-vision. How many more were doing the same?

Suddenly, I was worried about Rikki. Where she was hiding should have been far enough away from the fence line, but now, I didn't think it would be. She wouldn't know she was a sitting duck.

My best odds were if I evened them between all of us. I needed a set of those goggles and a gun. Stale cigarette-smelling bastard had both of those things.

The man moved quietly. Almost like a hunter—he likely was one. However, I stayed low and inched after him. My feet pressed down gently. Any pressure underfoot caused me to pause and find a different step.

Other than the rank nicotine odor, this man had developed skills out here. He didn't move fast, but everything was diligent. In truth, he might be more efficient without the night-vision. Now he had no peripheral view, and even when he turned back to survey the area I crouched, everything he saw was like staring down a tunnel. His scan crossed right over me without seeing me.

Too many times, people with good instincts relied too heavily on technology. There was only so much it could do. Instincts often went a lot farther.

I would tell him that if he stayed conscious. When I was within three long strides from him, I popped up with a quick advance. The figure jerked around at the sudden noise, and I caught him behind the neck, pulling him fast into the trunk of a hardwood. A crunch of glass and electronics echoed as the impact shattered the goggles on his face. He let out a yelp, but I slammed him into the tree again. The second blow rendered him unconscious—I guess he would not get the benefit of my wisdom after all.

Without missing a beat, I snatched the rifle the man had been holding. An AR-15. Bent over the figure, I checked the night-vision. The impact of face to tree trunk shattered the lenses. Testing them, I found they were useless.

At least I was armed.

I took off for the tree where I'd left Rikki. If I moved too fast, I risked running into another guard. This time, he might see me before I saw him. Every advance I made was meticulous, finding cover and staying out of the open. So far, no one shot at me.

Then I froze. Voices drifted through the woods.

"I have the girl," someone said.

A radio crackled. "What's your twenty?"

"Northeast of the fence. About a hundred yards."

The radio responded, "Is she alone?"

"No one's here," the first voice replied. He must have directed his next question to Rikki. "Are you alone?"

"Confirmed," he said into the radio. "She's alone."

"Decker, can you assist?" the radio asked.

I dropped lower and ran toward the voices.

The man on the other end of the walkie-talkie repeated, "Decker? Come in?"

No answer, and I wondered if Decker was lying unconscious by a tree right now.

I peered around a tree and saw a figure standing over Rikki. The outline of an AR-15 appeared to be pressed against her head.

"Decker! Come in!" the radio chirped again. Then it said, "Do you have eyes on Decker, Caleb?"

"Negative," Caleb responded.

I raised the barrel of the AR, lining Caleb up in the iron sights.

"Everyone converge on Caleb," the voice on the other end of the radio demanded.

An unfamiliar voice answered, "Affirmative. On the way."

It was about to get crowded out here.

"Hey," I called across the trees.

Caleb turned toward me, and I squeezed the trigger. The silhouette jerked as the round tore through his neck. Rikki rolled away as he collapsed on top of her.

"Shots fired!" someone shouted.

"Rikki, get out of here," I ordered, as I twisted around.

Gunfire erupted as one of the approaching guards started firing wildly in the dark.

12

Bullets chewed at the trees around me, and I flopped to the ground behind the largest trunk. I hadn't checked the AR-15, so I did not know how much ammunition it was carrying. I waited until the muzzle flash illuminated the dark woods. My trigger finger squeezed gently to fire a short four to six-round burst. The first barrage did nothing as the flashes happened again. A second volley of bullets struck flesh. The sound was immediately recognizable—I was too familiar with it.

My arms bent, tucking the AR-15 against me before I rolled to my right.

"Baker's down!"

"Where is he?" another voice called.

Prone on the dirt, I stared out into the darkness, tracking the voices. So far I only distinguished two. If Baker was the one I'd just shot, that probably meant there were only five guys patrolling the woods.

"Found Dexter!" the second one shouted. "He's alive, but down."

Rikki had better be getting as far from here as possible. Now, I really wished I'd left her back at the campsite.

A movement crossed from one tree to the next. I judged it to be about seventy feet away. My sights moved slowly to follow the figure's last location. It moved again, and I squeezed the trigger.

The shadow dropped out of sight, and I scrambled for another position.

"I'm hit!" the man I'd just shot called out.

"We need backup!" the other voice hollered.

His plea reverberated from Caleb's radio. He was calling for help. How many men did the complex house? Enough to outgun me. They might not all have night-vision, but I didn't want to wait and find out who did. I scrambled to my feet behind another trunk. My head extended around, searching for any movement.

I'd bought Rikki a full five minutes to get away from here. Through the trees, the sounds of ATVs roared in my direction. Bright lights bounced through the woods, casting long, thin shadows flickering through the forest and reminding me of some alien abduction movie. Dark shadows slid back and forth, and I didn't want to stay put.

Both feet took off to the south in a sprint.

"Over there!"

A gunshot rang out.

It didn't knock me down, so I kept running. The ATVs pulled up to a stop.

The engines drowned out all the voices, leaving me unable to hear the men's responses. I assumed someone would rush the last guy I shot and Dexter back for medical attention. They'd want to find Caleb, too. Somehow, I didn't think that would keep them from coming after me.

Sticks cracked as I bolted through the trees into the darkness. At best, I made out some shapes on the ground ahead of me, and I stumbled twice over fallen limbs and brush. Thorns, growing up from the forest floor, whipped me as I dodged left then right, occasionally bouncing against a tree. Ragged bark scraped my shoulder as I squeezed past a live oak.

The lights of the ATV chased after me. If I turned to gauge how far they were, I'd lose sight of any obstacles in front of me.

The forest floor raised up ahead of me, lifting the trees higher. A mound of some sort. Possibly left over from Native Americans living here a thousand years ago, or it could be nothing more than a damned hill. Whatever caused it didn't matter. It would give me high ground.

Over my shoulder, I watched the lights growing closer. My hands clawed at the saplings and vines popping up along the slope as I scrambled up the hill. The engine died, and three men scattered away from the vehicle. I ducked on the rise as their shadows scurried into the dark. Their strategy was smart. The bright LED lights lit up the mound, but it made it impossible to distinguish where they took cover in the dark.

With a roll to my side, I pulled the magazine from the AR, checking the ammo. Without counting, I estimated twenty bullets left. An AR usually holds thirty rounds. I fired about nine earlier.

If I were these guys, I'd attempt to flank me. They might have night-vision, but the LED lights would render those useless. I assumed that was their intent, thinking I might have taken a pair myself.

The one thing I couldn't do was wait for them to come around behind me or bring in reinforcements to storm my position. My head cocked as I peered down the sights at the headlights of the ATV. While they splayed the lights up the hill, my muzzle flash would be minimal, but not completely invisible. I'd have to risk it.

A single round fired, followed by a clink of broken glass. The right headlight blinked out. I repeated the same shot at the left light. Only light remaining was still glowing brightly from a light bar across the top of the cab.

My first shot was to the far-right side of the bar. Even after a direct hit, the light continued to beam up at me despite a few diodes dimming out.

Three shots rang out in sequence. The earth in front of me exploded, spitting dirt and rock into my face. I rolled left, changing position. It wasn't an overly strategic ploy, and my next shot would give it away.

I'd hoped to hit the light bar near the connector, disconnecting it from the battery. My first shot didn't do that, but I wasn't sure which side had the wires powering the lights.

With a deep breath, I tried again, targeting the left side this time. The bullet hit the mark with a loud pop, and the lights blacked out just as the shooting started.

Quickly, I scrambled away from the edge of the ridge. It took me a second to realize only two people were shooting at me. They were providing cover for the third to move around to flank me.

I crawled away from my position and hurried across the mound, staying close to the ground. It took me a minute to find cover on the north side of the mound. From where I was lying, I didn't have a clean shot on the ATV, but they'd have to move around to find me, too. I had a nice straight line of sight across the peak of the hill, and if I was correct, one of them would be creeping up the hill.

The two on the west side ceased firing. Now they were wondering a couple of things. Did they hit me? Did I take cover? Or did I get away?

In the distance, I heard a canine howl. It was several miles away. A few hoots and chirps called out over the still screaming cicadas. None of the gunmen were talking.

It took the third guy another five minutes to crest the top of the hill. I watched his silhouette move cautiously toward the ridge where I'd been lying. The barrel of the AR-15 in my hands followed him. I could drop him with no problem, but during the last few minutes, I wondered where his buddies had moved. Once I pulled the trigger, I gave up my only advantage.

The figure on top of the hill gave a whistle, intending to mimic a bird. A response came from the other side of the mound. Then a second rang out at the bottom of the hill, just below me.

I remained motionless, taking slow, shallow breaths. The reigning King of the Hill moved around more, walking within ten feet of me. Silently, I let up a brief prayer that the mud caked over my skin and clothes helped me meld into the mound.

"I don't see him," the king blurted out loudly. It was an amateurish thing to do.

"Where'd he go?" the man below me shouted.

"Hell if I know."

"Must've slipped off the back," the guy on the far side of the mound responded as he ascended the slope.

The first guy on the hill pulled a radio out. "We lost the guy," he announced over the radio. "We think he's heading east from the Indian mound."

"Affirmative," the response came. "We got Dexter and Baker back. Baker's bad."

"Shit," the guy up top cursed. "What about Dexter?"

"Busted up pretty bad, but he'll make it."

"This little bastard shot out our lights. We won't be much good in the dark."

"Gotcha," the man on the other end of the radio waves replied. "We're sending three teams out now."

"Roger, we'll head back."

"Jake, the boss says he wants this guy alive."

"Alive," Jake replied with some surprise. "After what he did to Jace?"

"He said 'alive.'"

"Okay," the man on the hill said with resignation.

"Let's go!" he called to the other two men.

I listened as three sets of feet shuffled back to their ATV. When the engine started up, I waited still, counting off the seconds. Their leaving could be a ruse, hoping to put me at ease. Whoever was driving inched through the trees, hampered by the lack of headlights. That might also answer whether those three wore night-vision.

After two minutes, I raised my head, looking for the trap to spring.

Nothing. The only sounds were the bugs and nocturnal sounds of the wild.

After rolling to a seated position, I slid down the incline, wincing as rocks and sticks poked into me. As soon as I reached the bottom, I sprang up and ran to the south. If they sent a search party out for me, it sounded like they thought I headed east.

Rikki had better be somewhere safe. I'd lie low for a bit before heading back to the campground. There was no way of getting word to her, but she'd managed for several days on her own out here. I trusted she could manage a few hours. Hopefully, she knew I would do the same.

The same howl echoed from afar. I imagined the activity in these woods scared off most animals, but that wasn't always the case. A coyote wasn't a big worry for me. They usually had the good sense to stay away from people. Around here, these predators had plenty to devour that didn't outweigh them, so they weren't looking to take down a person. However, those rules of nature were far from tried and true. Even if it couldn't eat me, I didn't want teeth marks on me either.

When I was about half a mile from the mound, I changed directions, backtracking toward the complex. The terrain dropped again, and I thought I might be in part of that dried stream bed where Rikki and I escaped on the ATV earlier. After climbing down, I stepped into the open. The stars glinted above, and without the curtain of leaves, I could see a little better.

On the north side of the gulch, a dead tree hung over the edge. Time and buckets of rainwater washed broken branches and trash into a pile on the eastern side, creating a hide. I approached it slowly, in case something chose this as a good neighborhood for raising babies. The barrel of the AR prodded underneath the makeshift shelter. Nothing came running out. After dropping to my knees, I gave the nook a more thorough inspection—somewhat limited in the dark.

Once I satisfied myself that I'd be alone in there, I crawled into the burrow. My back rested against the muddy sidewall of the gulch, and I listened to the night. From where I was sitting, I could see anyone coming down the gully. Unless they looked directly in, they would hopefully miss me entirely.

Just to be on the safe side, I dug at the surrounding dirt, bringing up handfuls of moist earth. After reapplying, I felt the camouflage sufficiently covered me.

It was almost midnight. My head rolled back against the mud wall, and I closed my eyes.

13

The wine bottle skipped across the room, spinning end over end. The thick glass curved like a boomerang as it flipped through the air and collided with a bookshelf where it shattered a vase and three framed pictures of Tommy, Jace, and Lily when they were in elementary school. Gray Connors turned his head at the sound of the crash while Tommy remained still in the opposite corner from the ruined landscape of books and glass.

They had designed the house with the master bedroom on the second floor, with three other bedrooms, one for each of them. Typically, new house construction put the master on the bottom level so that as the homeowner ages, they didn't have to climb the stairs, but Carla wanted a balcony to look out toward the river. Gray added a fourth bedroom on the first floor to accommodate those considerations. Now it was Tommy's room. Jace's had been next to the Carla and Gray's bedroom, but separated by an enormous bathroom shared by Jace and his sister, Lily.

Gray looked sadly at the shattered frames that lay strewn on the floor. He glanced up to the landing above, which had been a place for his kids' imaginations to run wild over the years: castles, forts, and more. Once it became a make-believe boat, and Gray recalled catching Jace, leaned back in a chair with a straw in his mouth as he tossed his fishing lure into the den below. Gray tore the boy's ass up for the rips in the couch cushion below, caused by the dragging of the empty hook up after each of Jace's casts. He didn't even remember how many couches they'd had in that room since then.

"Who the hell are they?" Gray demanded again, shaking the remorse away.

Tommy shifted his weight nervously as he watched the man's face redden. His father had asked him the same question three times in the past ten minutes, and each time he felt a wave of dread wash over him. Now, as his father's outrage ebbed slowly, Tommy found himself with enough courage to respond.

It was the broken pictures, Tommy assumed. He didn't mean to hit them.

Even if his father's anger waned, there was no answer to his repeated query.

"They aren't tourists," Tommy offered.

"No shit?" Gray spat, his dark eyes narrowing to slits as he spun to face his son.

"They could be cops?" Tommy suggested warily. He stepped back a little after he asked the question.

Gray's heart was hammering in his chest. This could be it, he mused to himself. "Feds? DEA or FBI?"

"It would make sense," Tommy added. "The girl showed up first. I bet she was scouting it out—trying to pass off as a nature freak."

"I thought she was an archaeologist," Gray stated. "Didn't Ledoux and Carlton find her at the Florida State site?"

"Yeah," Tommy answered.

"Shit!" he murmured. "Those damned archaeologists. They started all this. Why can't they just leave the dead Indians alone?"

"I don't know, Dad." Tommy furrowed his brows and shrugged. "Think the guy's a cop, then? Someone called about her missing?"

Gray walked over to a phone, yanking it off the receiver before his fingers dialed numbers with ruthless speed.

"Who are you calling now?" Tommy asked, glancing at the clock on the shelf that read 12:30.

"Ledoux," Gray answered as the other line rang.

"Andy, it's me," Gray growled into the phone before the other man could answer. "Did anyone call about the girl?"

"Uh, Gray, it's late," Andy Ledoux mumbled sleepily into the phone while Gray clenched his jaw tight enough to grind his teeth.

"I don't give a shit what time it is!" Gray shouted into the phone. "Did anyone call about the girl?"

"The department?" Ledoux questioned, still trying to wake up.

"No, asshole, your house," Gray barked. "Of course, the station."

"Yeah, some guy called. He thought the cops arrested her for trespassing, and he wanted to bail her out," Ledoux answered feebly.

Gray's face twisted into a visage of pure rage as he took three steps back and forth along the cord of the landline before demanding: "Who?"

Andy Ledoux's voice squeaked. "I don't know. It's at the office."

"Listen to me, Andy. Could there be Feds running around here?" Gray asked, his face twisting into a dour expression.

"I haven't heard anything," he reported.

"Would you?" Gray demanded, pacing three steps until the cord on the landline stretched and turning to step the other direction.

"I should," Ledoux answered, his voice dripping with dread. "James would for sure." He paused for a split second.

"What?" Gray hissed.

"Well, if they were investigating the department too, it's possible they would keep us in the dark."

A wave of panic washed over Gray as he shouted into the phone. "Shit! Get your ass out of bed and find James. I need to understand what I'm dealing with over here."

Ledoux knew there was no questioning the order and simply replied, "Yes, sir!"

Gray slammed the receiver down with a crash, leaving only one command hanging in the air: "Call me back!"

He seethed with rage as he leveled his glare at Tommy. "That idiot doesn't know anything, and if the Feds are actually investigating Chief James and his department, they sure as hell wouldn't be telling us about it."

"So what do you think might be happening?"

Gray made a dismissive gesture in response to Tommy's question.

"What do we do then?"

"Find them both." His voice was razor sharp as Gray spoke. "Call out every last one of our local boys. There's a bounty on this lowlife and I want the woods crawling with our people. Anyone who has any sort of allegiance had better show up in those woods with a gun in their hands."

"How many guys do you want out there?" asked Tommy.

"Every single one," Gray spat angrily. "Everyone who owes this family something needs to hit the woods right now."

"Yes, Dad, I get it. How much for the guy who kills him?"

"Nobody kills him," a coarse, feminine voice announced.

Tommy spun around to see his mother towering above them, her frame wrapped in a robe like battle armor. Black tears ran down her cheeks as her eyes glowed red with vengeance. Carla Connors had moved beyond grief and was ready for war.

"I want the man who killed Jace brought before me." The demand was austere and fervent.

"Mom, is that really a good idea?" Tommy asked uneasily. "This guy seems pretty dangerous. He's no joke."

Her brow furrowed and rage surged through her veins like molten lava. "Of course he's no joke," she growled through gritted teeth. "He killed your brother. This man ripped the heart out of this family."

She snarled menacingly. "I said I want him brought to this house."

Tommy's gaze shifted pleadingly toward his father in a desperate plea for assistance. Gray only issued him a single hard nod.

"What will you do to him?" Tommy asked, his voice taut with tension.

"The Bible says we shouldn't take an eye for an eye," Carla Connors said, her tone cold and unforgiving. "I care little for the Bible."

"Mom—" Tommy started, but a sharp bark from his father was cut him off.

"Tommy, heed your mother's words!" Gray commanded.

Carla Connors gave him one firm nod before turning away, striding into her bedroom without a word.

Tommy's eyes burned as he glared at his father. "What's she going to do, Dad?"

Gray inhaled sharply and ran a hand through his hair. "I don't know," he replied in a heavy voice. "She has a lot of pain and anger inside her. It's not going to be easy for her."

"To what end?" Tommy marched across the room to where the three broken pictures lay on the floor. He picked them up and held them in his hands as he surveyed the shattered images. "It won't bring him back, Dad," he mumbled. "Or Lily."

Gray met his son's gaze steadily. "You don't have kids yet, Tommy. You can't possibly understand what it's like to lose a child. Maybe we should let your mother handle this in her own way. She's been through a lot lately and she's become tough as nails. We need to trust that she knows what she's doing."

Tommy shook his head in frustration. "I think it would be safer and easier for everyone if we just killed him and dropped him in the river."

"Easier isn't always best," Gray stated with a sense of resignation.

Tommy let out a sigh of dread.

14

The next several hours passed slowly. I slept in short bursts, staying just barely aware of my surroundings. Screams of engines echoed through the forest as the men zipped around on their ATVs searching for me and Rikki. At least, I hoped they were still looking for both of us.

My skin itched under the dried mud, and I was wondering what a shower felt like. I'd gone much longer without washing, but I hadn't liked it back then either. Even on a long sea leg, I might dip into the ocean for a quick rinse. It wasn't as effective as a hot shower, but it beat being coated in grime. Or mud.

After about three hours, I jerked awake as one of the Polaris two-seaters ripped down the gully. The passenger carried a spotlight he was strafing along both sides of the ravine. They were moving too fast to actually see much, but his light passed right over the hide. In fact, it crossed my foot. I hefted the AR-15 up in case they stopped to investigate.

They didn't. The ATV continued through the pass, and I relaxed my grip on the rifle. A few minutes later, the vehicle was out of earshot.

It occurred to me that if these assholes tried using something quieter than the hundred-plus-horsepower off-roaders, they might actually sneak up on me. If they were smart, they'd put several guys on the ground while they continued their rounds.

Ideally, I'd get complacent, only paying attention when the engine screams came near.

I hoped they didn't think that clearly.

Everything centered on those Quonset huts. Rikki saw people moving cargo, but she wasn't sure what.

The simple answer was drugs. It was profitable enough to justify building a complex like that.

What were they doing, though? Smuggling it into the country?

This stretch of Florida didn't have as heavy a law enforcement presence as around the southern tip, but it wasn't nonexistent. How would they get it here? Freighters didn't venture north of Tampa much. If they did, that would certainly garner attention.

It would take small trawlers running up to slip past everyone. It was a long run from Cuba and Mexico, though.

However, if they could make it work, it had good potential. Highway 98 wasn't far, and the Suwannee River was navigable for a bit inland. They could shoot runabouts upriver to various stops where their cargo could move to a car and head all over the state. Georgia was only a few hours north, and getting to Atlanta was just a few extra.

That explained how they could afford so many men patrolling around here. Like Rikki commented, if they were all from here, they might be all family. Close friends, at least.

Someone mentioned "the boss" earlier. That wasn't how one talked about relatives, though, and these guys weren't overly conscious about what they said over the airwaves.

It was a lot to consider. Right now, I wanted to rest a few more hours before I ventured out to find Rikki.

When I opened my eyes again, it wasn't quite dawn. The clock in my head told me it was approximately four thirty. I knew it was actually 4:24, but with nothing to prove it, the point seemed moot even to me.

An engine roared down the gulch, and I waited as a Honda four-wheeler ran past. He was moving steadily, but not racing. A more efficient search method than some of the others had done. When he passed, I watched. In the distance, more motors droned. Three. And they all had the same cadence as the four-wheeler. Smaller engines than the Polaris RZR Rikki stole earlier had.

Six minutes later, the same ATV rolled past again. Same speed. Only one guy driving. He had a 30-06 similar to the one I lost yesterday. When he disappeared the other way, I relaxed again.

Five minutes and forty-five seconds. He came back down the stream bed. His speed had fluctuated very little.

I guessed the other motors I heard were using the same tactic. Likely it was an attempt to pin me in.

When dawn hit, it would be a lot more difficult to move if they had more guys running patrols. All I could consider was how I would operate a search like this: search along the edge of a border, assuming the target was inside. If I had the manpower, I would shrink that perimeter down, either funneling the mark into the center or, at least, into where I wanted them.

Ironically, if this was the outer boundary, I was already on the line of it. I could sit here for a few days and wait until they gave up. Then I'd walk right up to their front door.

The problem with that was Rikki. I didn't know where she was. Or even what the outline of their imaginary border might be. Or, in truth, if that was even what they were doing. It was all the wild speculation of a mud-covered boat bum who was dreaming of a hamburger and clean hair.

My theories be damned, I had no intention of twiddling my thumbs around here, anyway. Patience was a virtue, and I, unfortunately, lacked that value. I'd spent plenty of time in my life waiting for the battle to come. Nowadays, I preferred to get it over with.

If this guy's routine was the same, I had about five minutes before he came back through. The butt of the rifle pushed into the mud as I used it to climb to my feet. My legs needed a few seconds to unfold after been curled into the cranny.

I ran the opposite way the patrol went. The dark sky was lightening as the Earth rotated around. Morning was breaking out in the Atlantic, and in a short time, the sun would come up here. For now, I had enough light to make out the contours of the land, including the hills and trees. Fifty yards from where I'd slept, a large, old cypress jutted out toward the center of the gully. The root ball stuck out after much of the dirt washed away with the river over the years. Now, it grew at almost ninety degrees across the gully.

It took me two minutes to scoot up, or rather, sideways, along the trunk until the foliage masked me. The four-wheeler rumbled as it came back along the gulch. I checked the AR and waited. The drop to the ground was about twenty feet. It was doable, but I didn't like it. Instead, I slid down one of the branches about eight feet until the limb bent beyond what I was comfortable with it doing.

As the patrol came closer, I dropped from the tree. The goal was to land with my legs spread a foot apart and my knees ready to absorb the impact. I'd made worse drops from choppers in full combat gear.

I landed thirty feet in front of the ATV. The rifle popped up as the man braked the Honda. The guy stared at me, dumbfounded. He was in his late thirties with a scruffy brownish-red beard and an odd-looking mole just under his right eye. With the universal throat-slashing sign, I signaled for him to kill the engine.

"I'm going to need you to get off," I ordered.

"Shit!" he muttered. "Don't shoot me."

"My suggestion is you do what I tell you then," I explained. "Let's start with your radio."

Mole moved to grab his radio.

"Slower!" I demanded.

He paused before making a deliberate motion to remove the walkie-talkie.

"Toss it to me."

The man threw it underhandedly at me, and I reached forward to catch it.

"Now the rifle."

The 30-06 hung on a leather sling over his left shoulder on his back.

"Wait," I ordered. "Put your right hand on the handlebar."

When Mole obeyed, I told him, "Take it off with your left hand. Only touch the strap. If your fingers even brush the stock, I'll blow your head off."

He nodded, reaching slowly back to the strap across his shoulder. Awkwardly, he lifted it over his head, careful to only touch the leather strap. Once it was off his body, Mole extended his hand away from his body, letting the 30-06 dangle as if it was a dead rat or dirty diaper.

With a nod, I ordered, "Drop it."

He released the strap, and the gun clattered to the dirt.

"What's your name?" I asked him.

"Clay. Clay Thomas."

"Okay, Clay, I'm assuming you've heard about me."

He nodded.

"Climb off. Away from the rifle. Then get on your knees."

"Please don't shoot me," he begged as he swung his left leg over the seat and slid onto the ground.

"What are they doing?" I asked.

"What do you mean?" he stammered, sweat beading on his forehead.

"What did they tell you to do?"

"I'm supposed to be looking for you. If I see you, they told me to call it in. Try to keep you on that side of the creek." He gestured toward the direction I'd come from last night.

"Have they found the girl?"

He shook his head. "Not that I've heard."

"Okay, Clay Thomas. Let's get down to it. Who's the boss here?"

He didn't answer.

"You don't want me to kill you, do you?"

"No, sir," he replied. "But I can't tell you anything. I don't normally work for them, but I know what they'll do if anyone talks."

My right foot stepped forward, and the barrel of the AR-15 loomed closer to Clay's face. I'd been in that position before. The diameter of the muzzle increased the closer one's view to an enemy gun was. Right now, poor Clay was likely facing down his very first armed combatant.

He trembled. "I have a family," he pleaded.

"What does that matter to me?" I asked. "You'd have corralled me into a pen to be shot, or worse. Did you worry about my family?"

"If I talk, they'll kill them first."

Clay showed a lot more courage than I expected. I let out a heavy sigh. If he knew that I would not kill him in cold blood, he certainly didn't act like it. His eyes quivered as he stared down the barrel of the gun. But he wasn't going to talk.

"Damn," I muttered. My torso whipped around, and I rotated the gun in a swift motion before cracking him in the head. Clay Thomas slumped to the dirt, unconscious.

As I stared at his body, I noticed he was a little bigger than me—most of it was fat. Still, it would work. I dragged the man up the bank and stripped his red plaid shirt off. I pulled his belt off his jeans and used it to bind him to a thick branch of the cypress tree. He'd be able to get free eventually, but once he did, he'd think twice about joining the search for me.

The shirt was a little big on me, but hopefully from a distance, anyone would notice the pattern and not lack of a beard—although the last couple of days left me with an ever-increasing amount of chin hair. The 30-06 fit over my shoulder, and I let the AR sit in my lap as I started the Honda.

Rikki was still out there, according to Clay. She should have made it back to the campground, but if they brought out an actual show of force, they wouldn't give it a cursory walk-through. They'd find her, and I needed to get there first.

I turned the four-wheeler around and thumbed the throttle, heading back in the direction I'd come. After the Honda raced down the gulch a quarter of a mile, a yellow and black side-by-side ATV bounced out of the woods ahead of me. That ATV sat higher than the others I'd seen and was certainly taller than the Honda I was riding. "Wildcat" was emblazoned on its side. The driver waved at me to stop.

15

The man in the Wildcat was alone, and his gestures were still friendly. I braked slowly, letting my hand rest on the grip of the AR.

Just gonna be a good ole boy until I couldn't.

"What's your name?" he shouted over the rumbling engines.

He felt like he was on a mission—checking on the perimeter watchdogs. Hopefully, he didn't know Clay personally. I hoped he at least had an idea who he was.

"Clay. Clay Thomas." I regurgitated the name exactly as its owner had done earlier.

Wildcat shut off his motor—he wanted to talk. I did the same, trying to stay in character. If this guy considered himself in charge somehow, I'd let him keep thinking that. It was always safer to let the enemy think they have the control. They wouldn't react irrationally as long as they were confident. It was panic that makes bad decisions.

The early morning suddenly became quiet again, with only the ticking of cooling motors.

"I'm Jake," he announced. "They said you weren't answering your radio."

I blinked, staring at the man who'd been only three to four yards from me last night. My hand pulled the radio I'd taken from Clay off my waist.

"Damned thing got drenched earlier," I remarked, motioning to myself. "Ran through a mud pit. The water looked shallower that it was."

"At least you didn't stall out," he pointed out. "Mr. Connors wanted to do a check if anyone'd seen this asshole."

I shook my head. "Nothing down here. I've been up and down this creek bed a dozen times. I don't think he came this way."

"I doubt it, but he's sneaky," Jake commented. "We had him cornered last night. Somehow, he slipped right past me. I think he is heading the other direction, but no one's seen a hair of him."

"He might be a ghost," I said casually.

Jake paused, staring at me for a second. Some inkling in his brain set off a small alarm, warning him that something was amiss. "How'd your shirt stay so clean?" he asked.

"I took it off earlier," I answered. "It was in the pack. Didn't stay in long enough to muck it up."

His eyes twitched from the 30-06 on my back to the AR in my lap. Jake reached for his own gun, an ACR he had resting on the seat next to him. Before he got his fingers on the grip, my AR lay across the handlebars.

"Don't do it," I warned. The tone of my voice harshened as I stared across at the man.

"Shit!" he murmured.

"People have been saying that a lot today. Now set it back on the seat and put your hands on your head."

"I'm an idiot," he muttered. "Damned clean shirt. How'd I not see that?"

"Good catch, though," I remarked. "Although I didn't slip past you last night. You were in my sights until you and your buds were out of earshot."

Jake's shoulders slumped, realizing he'd escaped last night only to fall in line with my rifle again.

"Get out Jake," I ordered. "And do it nice and slow. You might be running out of luck with me."

The man slid out of the Wildcat and stepped away from the vehicle.

"What happened to Clay?" Jake asked nervously. "You kill him like you did Hopper and Eric?"

"He's still alive. When he comes to, he will have a hell of a headache," I assured him. "Why do you people think you can shoot at a guy and he won't fight back?"

The man didn't respond.

I motioned for him to march to the edge of the gulch. "Sit down."

He started to bend down when I added, "Cross your legs."

"Like Indian style?" he asked.

"Don't be racist, you dick. Like a kindergartner." I snapped at him.

When he obeyed, I said, "Let's talk about Mr. Connors."

Jake dropped his head to his chest. His expression deflated. He'd given up the boss without even knowing it. So far, he wasn't having the best morning.

"Look, by the time I'm done, one of two things is going to happen. Either I'm going to be someplace clean, dry, sipping on a rum runner."

He stared at me. Finally, he asked, "The other thing?"

My eyes narrowed. "I'll tear whatever you guys have going on here down to the ground. Somehow, I don't think either of those choices will sit well with Mr. Connors. Now, you get to decide what is best for Jake."

The man didn't move. It was difficult to tell if he was thinking about what I said, deciding if he was going to run, or wondering if he could attack me and take me out. For his sake, I hoped it was the first one.

"You called him Mr. Connors, so I'm guessing you and he aren't related. Who are you?"

"Jake Benson."

"How long you been working for this Connors?" I asked.

Jake shook his head. "I went to school with Jace," he told me.

"I don't know who Jace is," I stated bluntly.

"He's the guy you killed," Jake replied.

I let out a sigh. "At this point, you will need to be more specific."

"Tommy said you drowned him in the river."

"Ah," I realized. "The one with the machete."

"I guess."

"Seriously, he planned to kill me and dump me in the river."

Jake didn't respond.

"It would benefit you and your friends to understand that once in a blue moon, you're going to run into someone who doesn't take to the idea of being killed and dropped off like garbage."

Jake only bowed his head. Perhaps he wondered if that would matter after today.

"Have they found the girl?" I asked.

He shook his head.

"I heard that Connors wants me alive. Is that correct?"

"Yeah."

"What about the woman?" I questioned.

"They say they didn't care what happened to her, as long as she never got out of the woods."

"You guys are a bunch of assholes," I groaned. "Are you just helping because I killed your friend?"

"No," Jake admitted. "They pay well. I used to have the hardware store in town. I couldn't keep up with the bills. Mr. Connors bought me out. He keeps this community from starving."

"With what? Drug money?" I asked. "Or is he smuggling something else through here?"

Jake squinted at me. "I don't actually know. Some of us figure it's drugs. That makes the most sense."

My head cocked. "As I understand you, Connors is the town's benefactor. How many other businesses is he floating?"

The man shrugged.

"Safe to assume it's more than your hardware store, though. Right?"

"Probably. It's kinda an unspoken thing."

"Of course it is," I quipped. "He slowly buys the locals' loyalty. It doesn't matter what he does after that, does it?"

Jake Benson didn't answer.

"You sold your soul, assuming you ever had one, for what, a medium income in a shitty backwoods Florida town?"

"I grew up here," he blubbered.

"What does that matter? I grew up in a shitty backwoods Arkansas town, and I got out. No, you're lazy. Or do you enjoy what you do? Killing strangers because they get in your way."

"It's not like that," he refuted.

"I'm sure. You're probably a deacon in the local Baptist church, aren't you?"

He huffed.

"What happens if you refuse him?"

Nothing.

"That's what I figured. Now move."

"Are you going to shoot me?" Jake asked.

"Were you going to shoot me last night?" I countered.

"Probably."

"All to keep your crappy life here. I guess with that mindset, I should kill you just so I can keep my own life."

"Uh—"

A chuckle slipped out of my chest. "Count your blessings. Today's your lucky day then," I told him. "If I don't see you again, I won't shoot you."

He let out a sigh of relief.

"I wouldn't get excited yet," I warned him. "You aren't getting off too easy. Take off your clothes."

The former hardware store owner turned around to stare at me.

"I didn't stutter. Did I?"

"No," he stammered, bringing his hands off his head to pull the t-shirt over his head.

"Throw them over there," I ordered, pointing the barrel at the ground.

He stripped down to his shoes. Tattoos covered his chest. Most of them seemed like an amalgamation of symbols and images that meant little to me. Birds, Latin phrases, initials—likely his kids.

"Shoes, too."

Resignedly, he kicked off the Timberlands he had been wearing. Jake Benson stood in front of me, bare naked. He waited for me to tell him what to do next.

"Which way is the compound?" I asked.

He pointed to the northwest.

"Is Connors there?"

"Probably not. He lives closer to Como. Just off the river."

"I suggest you run in the opposite direction from here. It doesn't matter where you go, but if I see you again, I won't ask you anything before I kill you."

He nodded.

"You understand me?" I asked.

Another nod.

"Say it?" I demanded.

"If you see me again, you'll kill me."

I smiled at him and gave a motion for him to run along. Jake glanced at the hiking shoes.

"Nope," I answered his unasked question. "You get one shot to get out of here alive. And it's bare ass naked."

When he realized it was his last chance, he turned and danced across the rugged ground. His feet bounced awkwardly around as he hurried into the woods.

"Watch out for the sun," I warned, laughing to myself. "It's a bitch if you don't protect yourself."

Jake didn't turn back. He stumbled up the dry creek bank, wincing as he hobbled over the terrain. I watched until I lost sight of the man's pale ass in the trees. His grunts and curses were still audible as he made an uncomfortable trek.

I turned back to the two vehicles and grabbed the pile of clothes. When I got to the Wildcat, I tossed them onto the passenger's seat. I felt through them, pulling out a cellphone.

My thumb swiped across the screen, and the phone prompted me with facial recognition, which immediately failed. It seemed moot. The screen showed it had no service. Even trying to access the emergency services, which could be done without passing the facial security, was unsuccessful. Another plus for a hidden smuggling operation—natural communication blackout zone. No one could call in or out from here.

I dropped the phone on the seat, pulling out the rest of Jake Benson's belongings: a wallet with twenty-two dollars, a lighter, and a pack of Marlboro Lights. The cash came out and slipped into my pocket with the 30-06 shells I confiscated from Hopper and Eric yesterday—more spoils of war. The cigarettes landed next to the cell phone. However, the lighter twirled between my right index finger and thumb.

With my left finger and thumb, I picked up the pair of boxers Jake left behind. After opening the gas tank on the Honda, I stuffed the shorts into the opening before lighting the bottom of the underwear. The flame devoured the cloth, and I hurried back to the Wildcat. It had a bigger engine, meaning I could get more speed out of it than the four-wheeler. Plus, it had the roll bar in case I flipped it trying to escape.

By the time I turned the wheel and gunned the throttle, the fuel tank ignited on the Honda. It wasn't a boom like the movies showed. There was a loud *whoomph* as the gas in the tank caught fire. I wondered how much would burn. Whatever it was, it would be enough to render the vehicle useless should Jake circle back.

The Wildcat bounced up the bank, rocking on all four tires as it leveled out in the forest. I gunned the throttle, heading through the trees.

16

The morning sun cut through the leaves like a scalpel, slicing its way through the forest skin to reach the earth underneath. Rikki shifted in the bough of an oak tree. The rugged bark pressed against her back, leaving an imprint of her night.

She'd lost track of how far she ran before bright lights appeared in the woods. Rikki called on her free climbing skills as she scaled a nearby tree. When the ATV drove directly under her, she waited until it disappeared before dropping to the ground.

After another hour of wandering in the dark, she found a different tree with plenty of foliage on its lower branches and thick boughs where she finally rested. The night passed uncomfortably as she listened to the ATVs running around searching for her and Chase. She intended on waiting until the early hours to slip out of the branches, hoping that the hunters might suspend the search as they grew more tired.

Unfortunately, she eventually drifted to sleep—much deeper than she planned. Now, she woke up, and the sun had already gotten up into the sky.

The tree seemed safe enough, but it would not be ideal for whiling away the hours. For one thing, nature was calling her, and the idea of answering it thirty feet above the ground left her feeling uneasy.

She wondered where Chase was. Given the increase in people searching the forest, it seemed likely he'd gotten away too.

Her hands grabbed a branch over her head, and Rikki heaved up on it, adjusting her position on the limb. Birds were chirping and singing about the morning. In the distance, a couple of engines screamed in different directions as if they were running around.

Those ATVs screamed so loudly. She counted her blessings, though. At least she knew where they were.

If no one captured or killed Chase, he'd be looking for her. They hadn't talked about a rendezvous, but the obvious spot was back at the campground.

Rikki imagined Chase had silently cursed her more than once during the night for not staying at the site like he wanted. She'd almost agree with him. The patrols with night-vision surprised her.

Whatever the operation surrounding those buildings was, the people behind it organized it oddly. They put money into the equipment, but the guys using it acted untrained. Even she recognized that.

What did they have in those huts?

It must have been valuable—or dangerous—given how they were defending it.

She climbed down the tree, dropping to the next branch below her. She paused, hearing movement in the woods. Rikki bent at the knees, making herself smaller and giving her a panorama of the forest floor.

Six men came into view. All of them carried rifles and sported sidearms. From her perch, Rikki watched them move. They'd spread out over about a hundred feet. She guessed that gave them each a ten-foot radius all around them to search.

None of them spoke, only signaling each other. The line of hunters marched past Rikki's tree. No one glanced up in her direction. When they were gone, Rikki slumped against the trunk, letting her legs dangle on either side of the branch.

Maybe no one was defending the buildings, Rikki thought.

If most of the people they'd seen around the huts were out combing the forests, it might leave the huts unguarded or, at least, only guarded by a skeleton crew. What better time to get inside and see what the hell was worth all this? She imagined stacks of cocaine or marijuana.

She should head to the campground. Chase would meet her there. At least with all these people armed and on the hunt, it meant they hadn't gotten to Chase yet.

The problem was those men were heading in the direction she'd need to go in order to get back. What would Chase do if she wasn't there?

Rikki knew the answer to that. He'd charge headlong toward wherever he thought she was. That would be the compound. If that was the case, it made sense to head that direction while the place might only be guarded by a skeleton crew.

Plus, she bet the gear the cops took from her was there. The research on Gasparilla wasn't much, but there was a knife she carried around that she'd like to get back. It was a gift from Sam. His commanding officer and friend presented the skean to Sam only hours before he was killed in a skirmish. When Sam recovered from the attack on *Talitha* last year, he told her that his fighting days were at an end. It was important that the blade go to Sam's mentee—Rikki.

Hand-forged from Damascus steel, the traditional weapon extended seven inches from the hilt of the carved antler handle to its tip. The smith who crafted the weapon etched the words *Sinn féin* into the blade. The phrase, co-opted by the People's Liberation Army, meant "we ourselves." Sam told her it was akin to the musketeers' cry of "All for one, and one for all."

Now that she had time to think about it, it pissed her off more.

"Damn it," she muttered, clambering down the tree.

That was the best place for Chase to find her, she decided.

As soon as her feet hit the ground, she dropped into a crouch. With feline grace, she stalked through the woods.

She had covered a quarter of a mile before voices drifted through the branches. Rikki scanned around for another tree to climb, and when she found the ideal one, she scurried low to the ground a few hundred feet. As she pulled up on the lowest branch, the sounds of another patrol grew more distinct.

With increased speed, she pulled up higher in the tree.

"Wait!" a man called out.

From her position, Rikki spotted only a couple of men, but she was certain there were at least six. The two she put her eyes on were almost frozen. Each of their heads rotated slowly, searching. One cocked his head as if he was listening to the trees.

"I don't hear anything," an unseen individual pointed out.

"There was something," the first voice told the group. "Like a stick breaking."

"Might have been a squirrel or something," another suggested.

Rikki slowly shifted her left arm around the bough. She wanted to get a closer look, but they must have heard her scampering up the tree. She didn't want to shake the branches too much. Even if they couldn't see her, it only took a barrage of gunfire blindly fired into the foliage to bring her down.

Keep calm, she told herself, taking slow, deep breaths.

And she waited, counting off the seconds in her head.

"Let's wait here a bit," the first man who spoke ordered.

A few mumbled unintelligible complaints.

"There's nothing here," one of the hunters remarked with some annoyance. "We need to finish up. I'd like to get back to work."

"What work do you have?" someone joked. "Everyone from Como is out here. No one is coming in to get their hair cut."

A barber, Rikki wondered.

"This is a little stupid," the barber snarled. "What does he expect us to do?"

"It's Gray Connors," another responded. "He expects you to bend over and let him shove it up your ass. What else?"

"I'm just saying that I didn't sign on to shoot a couple of tourists who crossed his path."

A new voice laughed sardonically. "The hell you didn't," the chuckler pointed out. "You didn't turn down the money he gave you when Carol was in the hospital. He didn't charge you rent for an entire year. Damn, Mike, you raved about the man at the time."

"That's not the same thing," Mike complained. "Yeah, he helped me out. I didn't know I was selling him my soul."

"Don't forget about Jason Wilkes," someone reminded him.

"Jason just moved away," Mike snorted.

"Without packing his stuff. He just left his car at the house."

"We don't know."

"Oh, I know. Gray Connors didn't like it when he told him no about that lawsuit with the trucking company. Gray didn't want any investigators coming out to look into the accident, and he made it go away by making Jason go away."

"You think he's going to kill me because I don't want to kill a couple of strangers?" Mike asked.

"Someone said that one of them killed Jace. I don't think it would matter to Gray anymore who he runs over."

Mike added, "I don't care. I'm not sure I can just gun an unarmed girl down."

"Then let's hope someone else finds her."

"What about the guy? He killed like three or four guys already, including Hopper."

"Hopper was a dick."

"Yeah," Mike agreed. "But he was tough. Can track a mouse through a field."

"Could," someone corrected.

"Let's get moving. If Tommy checks our progress, I want him to think we're on top of it."

"Guys, what we said here—" Mike began to ask.

"We don't talk about it, understand?" the first voice ordered sternly. "No one rats to the Connorses in this group, got it?"

A murmur of agreement occurred before the men started their trek through the leaves. Rikki stayed in the tree. Now that she heard the talk, she grew more worried. These weren't just soldiers or minions. They were definitely untrained locals armed to kill—some without the stomach to go through with it.

She sat in the nook of the tree, remembering the last time she'd been with Chase. She saw what he was capable of doing. But she knew him. Chase didn't like killing people, but he had no problem with it, assuming he felt it was a kill-or-be-killed situation. A barber like Mike wandering through the woods, armed with automatic weapons, might constitute in Chase's mind, or rather, his instinct, as a kill-or-be-killed scenario.

She wondered if Chase would justify it. Everyone had a choice. Some people just didn't make use of it. Mike and the others could have turned down this Gray Connors. Instead, they took up arms to hunt Chase and Rikki down.

Her stomach growled, and she remembered the handful of raspberries from last night. Right now, a big plate of pasta sounded perfect.

She groaned, annoyed at the predicament. Her ears listened for more hunters. The group that stopped under her tree was long gone. She swung down, branch to branch until she dropped to the ground. Her knees bent slightly, absorbing the impact as she landed perfectly on her feet.

Again, Rikki made her way from tree to tree until she saw the chain-link barrier around the compound. Three men stood on the eastern edge of the fence, each stationed about thirty feet apart and staring out into the woods.

Rikki moved slowly around the compound so she could come up on the western side. The only way onto the other side of the fence was over it. At the top of the chain link, three strands of barbed wire stretched across the opening.

Scaling the fence part was easy.

At least it's not razor wire, she considered as she attempted to swing her leg over the barbed wire.

Sharp points sliced through her inner thigh, and Rikki sucked in a gasp as she rolled over. The front of her shirt snagged on the barbs, as she threw herself off the top. A rip sounded as she fell from the fence. Instinctively, she curled into a ball, slamming into the ground in a roll and protecting most of her body.

As she sat up, she gave a cursory inspection for severe damage. Her legs and arms bore thin red streaks from the barbed wire, and a slit formed on her chest, coursing at an angle from her right breast to the bottom left.

No one seemed to see her, and she made a mad dash for the building. As she skirted along the side, Rikki checked for any guards.

So far, the small contingent wasn't alerted to her presence. She paused at a man door. Her hand reached over to test the handle. As she turned it, the door swung open suddenly.

Rikki stepped back as a man appeared in the doorway holding a twenty-two-caliber pistol at her head.

17

I pulled the Wildcat off to the side of the trail and cut the engine. Before I ventured on, I wanted to come up with a semblance of a plan. As far as weaponry, I was well-stocked with the AR-15, ACR, and the 30-06. The AR had twenty-eight rounds. The ACR's magazine was full, with twenty-four bullets, and for the 30-06 I had eighteen cartridges, most still in my pocket.

If a couple of guys from my unit joined me, we would clear the compound in time for lunch. That was only a bit of an exaggeration, but my confidence would be much higher. So far, none of the men I'd encountered would put up much of a fight against three Marines.

Unfortunately, it was just me. I hoped Rikki got back to the campground safely. Where did the camp fall in Connors's search perimeter?

At the moment, I struggled with which way to go. With the Wildcat, I could cover a lot of ground fast. I might not outrun all of them, but given the firepower sitting in the seat next to me, I could hold them off—especially if Rikki drove and I manned the gun.

It was a long run to the campground and back, though. What if she didn't make it back there? I'd waste a lot of time trekking over there. Even if I wanted to find her, that didn't leave me a lot of ground to search. Or rather, it left me with too much ground to search. Rikki had had a couple of days to learn the land—where to go to ground. Unfortunately, I didn't know where she'd go other than the campground.

Or the compound.

Even if Rikki sought the safety of the camp, it had been nearly twelve hours now since we separated. How long would she wait there for me?

She was one of the smartest and most self-reliant women I knew—and I knew a few. I didn't think she'd wait too long before going out on her own. She might assume something happened to me if I didn't make it back, and that would likely spur her to head out.

To the compound.

If Jake and Clay were correct, then the Connors clan sent everyone out on the prowl for me. That meant the Quonset complex wouldn't have that many guards there. At least, that made sense to me. If that were the case, I might infiltrate the buildings and figure out what the hell was going on here.

When I was done today, Connors would wish he and his family had left me alone.

I started the engine on the Wildcat and aimed it in the direction of this secret whatever they were trying to hide out here.

The trails along the river zigged and zagged in different directions. I knew I needed to head west from the dry creek. While I knew the directions, three times I found a different trail that arced away from the compound. Every one of the wrong turns ate up minutes as they forced me to backtrack.

At one point, I passed four men walking grid-like patterns in the trees off to the right. The closest man offered a wave as I drove by. No one told them to expect me on an ATV. I remembered what Rikki mentioned, that none of them seemed to think for themselves. Connors amassed a small army of

Florida rednecks that could only do what they were told. A few, like Jake, might have the wits to do more, but even he wasn't made for this kind of work.

It was an interesting thing to note that in almost any conflict, both sides usually had a foregone conclusion that their side was going to prevail. That mindset could dull the senses and leave an opening for the enemy. As a Marine, I knew the end was victory, while understanding that the fight was ours to lose.

When I finally spotted the compound, I didn't bother slowing as I approached. Two men stood on either side of the gate staring out with a blasé look on their faces. Boredom was the segue to complacency. Some people might mistake it for stoicism like the no-nonsense duty of a military guard, but the eyes told a different story. Their faraway gaze seemed locked on places nowhere in their periphery. A Marine on guard had a fixed stare ahead of him, examining everything in 180 degrees. They were determined and prepared while the bored ones were vacant.

Today, their boredom lifted my spirits. A two-finger wave at the one on the right allowed him to slip back into this catatonic state.

I steered the Wildcat to the left, having seen a group of three men posted along the opposite stretch of fence. From here, I couldn't tell how efficiently they took their duty. Best to take it around the other way, where fewer prying eyes seemed to be.

I braked suddenly. Two hundred feet from me stood Rikki trying to open a man door.

The door swung open, and the kid with the twenty-two pistol stepped out. He leveled the same gun at Rikki's head. I reached for the 30-06 when the man lifted his eyes my way. Even at this distance, I noted the glimmer of recognition.

With a swift motion, he caught Rikki by the hair, dragging her into the building as the pistol fired my direction. At that distance, he wasn't getting close with a short-barreled handgun combined with his increased panic. The rifle came up to my shoulder, and I squeezed the trigger. The first round banged into the door as he ducked behind it. I fired another crack and smashed my foot to the floor. The Wildcat jerked forward as I pulled the trigger again. That last round missed its mark, but Twenty-two's shot whizzed past my head.

I spun the wheel right, and the ATV pivoted around in a semicircle. Ahead of me, the guards previously engrossed in complacency were now fully in the moment as they charged my direction, firing their weapons at me.

"Dammit!" I cursed, turning the Wildcat into a skid. Dirt and debris sprayed up like a rooster's tail behind a water-ski.

Twenty-two retreated into the building with Rikki—good luck for me as I aimed the ATV past the man door. My fortune completely changed as the man door burst open and three guys charged out with automatic rifles.

I dropped the barrel down and it hit the floor next to the accelerator. As soon as I let go, I snatched the AR-15, raising it and squeezing the trigger. The Wildcat ripped past the three gunmen, peppering them as I flew by them. At least one of them fired a burst of gunfire that seemed to miss me.

The gas pedal pressed down as I raced toward the rear of the building. Gunshots sounded behind me. In the rearview mirror, I counted five men firing at me. My head ducked as the back of the ATV caught several rounds.

Again, I took a ninety-degree bend around the Quonset hut. A second later, I repeated the turn to cut between two buildings. Somewhere I heard the scream of more motors very near to me.

In front of me, a guard ran across the opening between the buildings. He stopped in the center of my path, lifting his own AR-15 to fire. The Plexiglas windshield peppered with bullets leaving peck marks. When I didn't stop, he took aim again. For a split second, it was a contest of chicken. The instant before the ATV was on top of him, he realized I wasn't stopping.

The wheels bounced with a resounding crunch as the front plowed him into the ground and the back tires crushed his skull. It seemed senseless, but he'd played a game he couldn't win—that wasn't my fault.

As the Wildcat ran over the guard, I raced from between the buildings, glancing to my right where the five guards watched their compatriot mowed down. It was enough time to aim for the gate. To my left, the cry of a posse caught my attention. Three ATVs, like the Polaris and Wildcat, zoomed toward me. I had an instant to discern the passenger in the lead vehicle hanging around the windshield with a gun firing at me.

The forest engulfed me as I emerged from the complex. Immediately, I twisted the wheel right, zipping off the trail for a second. A gunshot exploded behind me, and I cut to the left around an oak tree. My tires crossed the threshold of the fence line to the thicket of trees.

All three of the ATVs stayed with me as I weaved around the trees like they were buoys on a slalom course. I needed to get rid of them, but they had me outgunned. My only option was to outmaneuver them.

I feinted to the left before jerking the wheel right. The rear left tire ricocheted off a pine tree, sending me into a slide perpendicular to my pursuers. The AR came up in that instance. With precision and an intense amount of luck, I shot the passenger in the lead vehicle. Before I got control of the Wildcat, he snapped back, falling off the ATV. The driver didn't stop, and the other two vehicles arced around the fallen gunman.

Checking my rearview mirror, I watched the two rear ATVs split in opposite directions. They weren't about to let me make another move like that. By flanking me, they'd cut me off from whichever direction I tried to break toward.

The lead vehicle pressed on my ass. He was planning to ram me, and I pulled the wheel back and forth taking the Wildcat in an S course. He tried to stay with me, but it wasn't quite exact. When I slammed the brakes, he almost flew past me before he hit his brakes. He soared up alongside me in that split second, and I shot him in the head.

The other two ATVs were several seconds behind me as I took the rapidly slowing Wildcat into a skid that spun me around. By the time they followed me in a complete turnaround, I gained a hundred yards on them.

I didn't hear the gunfire, but the roll bar rang as bullets struck it. No way was I going to slow. With a head start, I wasn't about to let them have an inch, and I drove furiously.

More gunshots. This time, I heard them as they hit the back of my ATV.

Burning oil seared my nostrils. They hit something, and if I was losing oil, it was only a matter of minutes, maybe seconds, before I lost power. What I needed was a defensible location. The problem was it wouldn't take long for reinforcements to get here. I estimated they were already on their way.

Gunfire again.

A pop sounded in my left ear as the Wildcat rotated around at full speed. Some part of my brain registered the tire blowing as the ATV continued forward while the sudden loss of a wheel twisted it around. As if it were in slow motion, the world tumbled around me as the wheels came off the ground.

Since the seatbelt strapped me into the driver's seat, I wasn't being thrown from my seat. However, my arms and head flailed as the vehicle twirled through the air. The first impact snapped me like a whip as the Wildcat slammed into the dirt on its rollbar. It continued to roll, bouncing around three times before crashing into a tree.

The roll bar over my head bent under the pressure of the earth and tree. For a split second, I glanced up at the chewed-up bark of a cypress tree. I realized the creased steel tubing embedded itself in the wood. Then, everything faded away to darkness.

18

Before I opened my eyes, I noticed the scent of burning oil wasn't there. Something else was burning.

A candle?

My eyelids took a considerable effort to force open. They wanted to just close again for a few more minutes. Sleep begged me to join it.

You aren't asleep, asshole.

I forced my lids open again.

I wasn't sleeping—but I was in bed.

No, it wasn't a bed. I was on my back, staring at an old popcorn ceiling with a slight tint of age.

With a deep breath, I sniffed, searching for the cigarette odor. There wasn't any. Instead, it was cookies. Or maybe it was vanilla.

Everything hurt, though. My chest ached and my head throbbed. Both of my arms felt like I'd just finished one of the most intense biceps training days at the gym. It reminded me of rowing my dinghy for a couple of miles.

I tried to sit up, but my head only lifted a few inches before it stopped. Something pinned me down, and I tested my limbs. My upper arms were bound just above the elbow. Someone had also tied my legs down around my thighs. I twisted my ankles back and forth, but nothing else would move. The same for my wrists, although I had a little more play on my elbows than my knees.

Damn, my clothes are gone. That realization annoyed me more than being trussed up.

I lifted my head to survey my surroundings, pressing my chin against my chest. It was a bedroom of some sort. A girl's room based on the decor of colorful posters with unicorns and teenage boys who, I guessed, were some kind of teen superstars.

I wasn't on a bed. It was a table. At first I thought it might be an exam table, but my bare skin wasn't touching metal. It was plastic. My wrist contorted around until I tapped the surface. Definitely some type of plastic.

And a candle sat on a dresser by the door. When I read the label, I realized I was right. It was vanilla.

The door opened, and I lifted my head again to see the man I'd encountered on the island yesterday. Was it only yesterday? He was the one who struck me with the twelve-gauge.

Now that I had more than a split second to study his features, I saw he was in his fifties with crow's feet around his eyes. He carried himself as if he was the smartest person in the room. He offered a smug smile at me.

"Good, you're awake." His words seethed with condescension.

"You must be Connors."

When I mentioned his name, it startled him. "You're a cop?" he asked too fervently.

I held my tongue. That one question told me a lot. He didn't know who I was, but he'd already suspected I might be law enforcement. It might mean he'd weigh whatever happened next differently if he thought I was a cop. Of course, the big question was whether that supposition would play out in my benefit or not.

"Doesn't matter." He recovered his swagger. "If you'd called for backup, they'd already be here. If you had reported what happened so far, we'd have Feds pouring out of our ears."

So much for it benefiting me.

"You brought out quite the welcoming party," I remarked. "Doesn't that seem a little ridiculous?"

Connors scowled at me. "There was a chance for you to get out of here alive," he suggested.

My head shook. "Not the way I saw things," I corrected. "Long before I killed Jace, you and your boys planned to drown me in the river."

The man couldn't stop the second register of surprise across his face when I called his son by name.

I mustered a smug grin to match his face. "Come on, Connors. You have misjudged me at every turn."

"You are a cop," he surmised.

"Don't be dumb! If you murder an officer of the law, your problems don't go away," I pointed out. Common sense would have told him that. Plus, Connors struck me as a conniving son of a bitch. He'd also know that a missing or dead agent would bring more attention. However, the truth was there was little reason to leave me alive. Right now, I knew enough about his operation—as little as that was—to bring a world of trouble down around him. If I were a cop, the most logical thing to do was to kill me. He might have time to move his product out of the buildings, suspend his business, and wait out any legal issues that might come his way. He didn't even have to do that here. If no charges were levied against him, it would be smart to give time for the dust to settle in a nice, tropical country with little to no extradition treaty with the United States.

He sneered again at me. "I'm willing to bet that you haven't passed enough up the chain to cause me any problems."

Connors continued, "In fact, I figure it all started with the girl, right? That's the first thing you asked when me and the boys ran across you on Turkey Island."

"I don't get it though," I commented. "You did not know what we were doing, but you drag everyone out on the hunt. It's overkill."

"Overkill?" he stammered. "You killed my son."

"Now, that wasn't entirely my fault," I suggested. "We both fell overboard."

Connors leaned into my face. I pulled my head away from his hot breath. "You both went into the river, but only you seem to have come up."

"You told him to kill me," I said. "It's not like I had any intention of just letting him do that."

"That will be your last mistake," he hissed.

During my first tour in Afghanistan, I was driving into a village in the north where a Taliban stronghold was located. My only job was to drive and provide exfiltration and backup. Lieutenant Davidson, the unit leader, gave some wise words to the men before we engaged. He said, "Marines don't cower. If a Marine is backed in a corner, it's time to double down."

I considered that remark as I stared into Connors's fire-red face, and I doubled down. "I think that was Jace's last mistake."

He let out a growl, pulled back, and hit me in the face. My head slammed into the table with a dull *thud*. "Don't you talk about my son, you bastard."

"You killed him just as much as I did," I suggested. "This method of wiping anyone off the board that gets near your toys only works if you don't hit any opposition."

"Is that what you are?" he questioned. "Opposition?"

With a jerk toward him, I stretched my head as far as the binds on my arms allowed me. "Connors, I'm the 'find out' that comes when you 'fuck around.'"

My quick lunge startled him, and he jumped back. In less than a second, he recovered, driving his fist into my face again. Blood drizzled down my cheeks from my nose, and Connors straightened up. A stoic mask slipped over his face, and he adjusted the front of the button-down Izod shirt. The man turned slowly, walking out of the room and leaving me alone.

With no one in the bedroom, I focused my attention on my restraints. The ropes were thin paracord, but the knots were the constrictor type. Every time I tugged against them, the lines tightened, pulling against the skin. Those styles of knots worked like the old Asian finger cuffs. The more I struggled against them, the more it pulled against itself. The method used my strength against me.

Whoever secured me to the table did so with some masochistic tendencies. If I relaxed, it almost felt like I could pull my arms free. In fact, there were a few inches of wiggle room going up and down my biceps before I had moved too much, and the bind tightened.

My elbow would bend, and by contorting my arm into an extremely uncomfortable angle, I thought I could almost reach the cord. I was three inches too short. Over the next few minutes, I wiggled and squirmed, trying to find those few inches of leeway in the rope. Each time I'd shave off an inch, the ropes dug into my flesh until I couldn't move. My elbow eventually dropped, and my hand collapsed beside me.

At this point, I didn't know how much more doubling down I could do. There needed to be an opening before I could do anything effective.

After several seconds, I picked my head up to scan the room again. Outside the window stood a live oak—at least the upper branches of one. It put me on the second floor. It was impossible to see what the roofline looked like, but the angle of the ceiling indicated the roof sloped past the window. I could jump about eight feet from the house to a lower branch of the tree—assuming there was at least one thick enough for me to catch or land on. From there, it could be a quick descent down.

Unless someone sealed the windows shut. From where I was lying, I noticed several painted heads of nails along the window. Each toenailed at an angle. Connors didn't want his daughter sneaking out or someone sneaking in. That was obviously an old feature, as several of the nails now had only flaking paint covering them.

Of course, I could break the glass and scale out. That might be better than making my way through the house.

Something bugged me about being locked in the daughter's room. Surely, a teenage girl would balk at someone being murdered in their room.

I took another slow look around the bedroom. The tables and shelves were dust free. I didn't see any clutter—no signs of someone living there at all. Even the wastebasket was empty.

It wasn't a room, after all. Connors kept this as a shrine.

The door opened, and I turned my head to see if Connors returned. It wasn't him standing in the doorway.

Instead, a woman in her fifties silhouetted the space. When she stepped forward, I studied her face. Exhaustion filled it. Her eyes were vacant but red. She wore a floral smock and carried a small handbag as if she might be about to head to the store.

"Help me," I pleaded. "You need to let me out."

"I can't do that," the woman uttered in a husky tone. "You can't leave."

"Listen to me," I urged. "You must be Mrs. Connors. Your husband is making a terrible mistake. It's going to get more people killed."

"More people?" she asked, her voice seeming to soften.

"Yes. No one else needs to get hurt," I explained. "He's let it go too far."

"Yes," she replied. "It's gone too far."

I didn't respond to her. Her eyes were no longer vacant. They transitioned from a pitiful stare to sullen and then, in a flash, to rage.

"It's only too far when you think you are going to die," she scolded. "When you killed my baby boy, it wasn't too far, was it?"

"You know he was trying to kill me, right?"

Mrs. Connors set the bag down near my knees. My neck craned to watch as she removed a scalpel with about a two-inch blade.

"What are you doing?" I demanded.

She smiled a faint grin at me. "Oh, don't worry," she assured me. "I don't plan to kill you."

We stared into each other's eyes with intensity.

"Yet," she added. "Before that, though, I'm going to make you wish you were dead."

She lifted the scalpel with the flourish of someone who had no misgivings about what was coming next.

19

"Aargh!" I screamed as Mrs. Connors meticulously peeled the skin from my muscle.

I'd tried to hold in the pain, but the woman took great pleasure in making sure I felt it. She doused the area with alcohol. The searing agony arched my back as I instinctively struggled to get away. She pulled on the paracord, holding me to the table. Her face offered a satisfied smirk when she knew the binds weren't loosening despite my struggles.

"I imagine that hurts," she whispered as she used the scalpel to flay a small section on my chest. "I've read that the ethanol will actually impair the healing of a wound. The pain receptors in the body can't distinguish the burning sensation from the original injury."

Her voice remained impassive—almost sterile—as if she were describing an autopsy.

"Who knows if it's true?" she mused. "It won't matter in your case."

I hissed air between my teeth as I attempted to focus on my surroundings. I'd undergone various methods of torture in SERE School after being assigned to Recon. The Survival, Escape, Resistance, and Evasion training that made up SERE involved sleep deprivation, hypothermia, and dehydration. Most of those things were actually illegal under international laws, but as one trainer pointed out—laws didn't mean shit to the enemy.

None of that preparation included being skinned alive, either.

Mrs. Connors should teach classes on it. She'd restricted the area she was working on to a few inches square. It kept the pain in an acute spot, making it seem worse.

"That must sting," she remarked as casually as someone knitting a sweater. My face winced as she tore the flesh from the muscle.

"I'm going to make you regret this," I breathed out as she paused long enough to pour more alcohol over the wound.

"That seems unlikely," she retorted, and I ground my teeth together as the antiseptic scorched the open lesion. "At this point, you should be regretting your choices."

When I let the last gasp out, I snarled. "You are a crazy bitch!"

"That's what happens when someone takes your son away."

"Your son tried to kill the wrong person," I snapped back. "You're making the same mistake."

Her index finger tugged on the paracord, cinching it around my arm and cutting off the circulation. The rope twanged.

"There seems to be very little you can do about it," she suggested smugly.

The door to the room opened, and I strained my head to see who was there. Twenty-two stood in the opening. He locked eyes with me for a split second before his gaze drifted to the flap of skin peeled back from my chest.

"Where is she?" I shouted at him. He was the last person I'd seen with Rikki, and when I got out of here, I intended to find her.

The woman laughed. "The girl is the last thing you should be worrying about."

"Mother," Twenty-two interrupted. I glanced between the two. He was the second son—younger than Jace.

"Can you come downstairs for a minute?" he asked her.

Exasperated, she stared down at my chest as if she hadn't quite finished putting together the puzzle she'd been working on.

"One second Tommy."

"I guess you get a short reprieve," she told me.

A quick breath escaped my lips. In a swift, fluid motion, the woman ripped the flap of skin off like a bandage. My eyes watered as I felt the sinews of flesh rip away like Velcro.

The nerve endings overloaded with agony, and my head swooned just as the bile forced its way up my throat. With considerable effort, I slung my head to the side, spewing stomach acid onto the table.

"How unbecoming," Mrs. Connors told me, grimacing as she rose to her feet.

I never heard the door close. Instead, I tried to control the anguish. After several seconds, the spasm subsided to an aching burn. My neck relaxed, and my head lolled over with exhaustion.

The only thing I wanted to do was pass out, but that would not help me at all. Seconds ticked by in my brain, turning into minutes. After ten minutes passed, the door opened.

"You're awake?" Mrs. Connors announced with some surprise. "I'm impressed. It seems my husband and son want me to finish you quickly. They both seem to think you are a government agent. Is that true?"

"Would it matter?" I rasped.

"To me?" she responded. "Only slightly."

"As long as you get your pound of flesh?" I asked, considering that she intended to take that saying literally. "It won't bring your son back."

"Don't talk to me about Jace!" she shouted.

"Okay, what about your daughter?" I questioned. "Can we talk about how she died?"

Mrs. Connors's face soured. "Don't you dare talk about her!"

"She's dead, though. Right?" I pushed harder. "I can't imagine a teenage girl wouldn't throw a fit about you dissecting a human in her room. You've kept it like she left it, didn't you? Was it suicide?"

The woman growled as she picked the scalpel up. Her eyes narrowed to shark-like slits as she focused on me. "How about I take something of yours?"

Her focus drifted to my arm where my tattoo was. The design was a skull and crossbones commemorating the Marine Corps, only the traditional crossbones were replaced with an oar and a knife. I got the tattoo during my first leave from Parris Island. Barely eighteen, it was the branding of a new life for me. No longer was I Chase Gordon, some shithead kid from Arkansas who endured countless abuse from his father. I came out of Parris Island a new man, and that ink was my birthmark.

It didn't matter that I left the Corps. No one ever really leaves the Marines. It's like a hometown—you can travel as far away as you can, but it's still home.

Mrs. Connors leaned over my shoulder, studying the artwork.

"Marines, right?" she asked. "Gray was a Marine, too."

I fixed my face into a scowl.

"I'll tell you what," she offered. "Why don't you tell me who you are? Who you work for? In exchange, I will save the tattoo. Keep it intact. I could even drop it in the mail to your mother. Something to remember you by. It's more than you left me of Jace."

I laughed. It wasn't even a cynical chuckle. It was a full-on laugh.

"What do you find so funny?"

"That you would probably discover my mom to be exactly like you—a sociopathic bitch. She couldn't give two shits if I was alive or dead. I mean, she'd do all the proper mourning for everyone to see. But it's all fake. She wouldn't care."

I added, "Just like you don't actually care about Jace. Or your daughter. This is your own pride. You're worse than a crazy bitch. It's selfish. It makes you the absolute worst mother—I'd know, mine comes in close. How do you allow your boys to get involved in all this? It's inevitable that one or both would die doing it."

"How dare you talk to me that way?"

"See, you don't deny it," I pointed out. "You only want to maintain control. I thought my mom was bad."

Rage filled her face, and she brandished the scalpel like a trophy. The blade was razor sharp, and the first cut felt as if she was tugging against the skin. She began cutting around the tattoo as she'd done on my chest. It was like scoring a piece of paper. Only I was the paper and I bled.

She inched closer to my shoulder as she struggled to make a straight cut.

My neck whipped toward her. I struck her in the nose with my forehead. The first blow took all my effort, and the strike caused her to jerk back, dropping the blade as she reached for her broken nose. Warm steel landed on my abdomen, and I snatched it with my left hand. My forearm stretched across my torso as I tried to cut the cord on my right bicep.

As the constrictor knot tightened, the cord cut into my skin while I swiped the blade across my arm. The edge sliced into my flesh, but it didn't sever the cord through.

Suddenly, the woman's hand grasped my wrist, struggling to wrestle the scalpel away from me. I wrenched it away, slashing the rope again. She grabbed my fingers, and I strained against the cords holding me down. The woven fibers dug into the skin with more pain than the blade's cuts had caused.

My left arm struggled against her, and then I snapped it toward her. Already pulling hard against me, Mrs. Connors wasn't ready for me to push into her. The arm flew back, and I sliced at her fingers with the blade.

I felt the paracord pop on my right bicep. The blade hadn't severed it, but it sliced through several strands, weakening it. Now free, my right hand swung across my body, forming into a fist, and struck Mrs. Connors in her already broken nose.

She let out a furious shriek, and I switched the scalpel to my right hand. The cord on my left arm cut like butter, and I caught the woman by the hair as she turned to flee for the door. With a quick lurch, I drove the blade into her throat. A spurt of blood erupted as I pulled the knife free.

The crazed woman stumbled two steps toward the door before collapsing. With a flick of my wrist, I cut my left leg free.

As I moved to the rope on my right leg, the door flew open and Tommy Connors stood in the doorway. For a second, he stared at me, half-sitting up. Then he saw his mother in a pool of blood.

"No!" he shouted.

I sliced the other cord as he lunged at me. The two of us rolled off the table, falling onto the shag carpet. The kid threw wild but powerful punches, and I blocked them as we tussled on the floor. My legs wrapped around his waist, and I tossed him to the side. The scalpel dropped during our fall, but we upended a small table holding a unicorn lamp and a clock radio.

The lamp drove into his face, shattering on impact. Shards of glass embedded in his cheeks and eyes. I grabbed the radio and jerked the cord from the wall. Tommy struggled to get out from under me. Both of my hands wound the power cord around his neck, pulling the loop tight and cutting off his supply of oxygen. He flailed like a dying fish, trying with one last gallant effort to make it back into the water. Only for Tommy, there was no water.

His hand reached back to the gun in his waist. As he tried to pull the twenty-two-caliber pistol free, I took both ends of the cord in my left hand. My right hand caught his wrist, slamming it to the ground before he could get the barrel up to fire. The cord twisted in my grip, crushing his esophagus.

"What the hell?" a voice shouted from the hall.

I grabbed the twenty-two from the floor and twisted around, pulling Tommy up with the clock radio cord. A uniformed cop stood in the door to the room. His hand came up to his belt to pull his thirty-eight revolver from his holster. Within a breath, I shot him between the eyes. Tommy continued to gyrate as the officer fell to the ground.

The barrel of the pistol remained trained on the door as Tommy Connors slowly stopped fighting, the life twitching out of him in small spasms.

Thirty seconds passed before I stood up and let the kid's body slump to the floor.

Blood dripped down both arms and my chest. On the dresser by the door, I saw the two-inch square of skin Mrs. Connors ripped off my torso. In the mirror attached to the dresser, I stared at myself standing naked with a pistol in one hand.

20

I took a deep breath, staring at myself in the mirror and listening at the door for more men to charge in the room. The house had an eerie quiet to it, and after I counted off thirty seconds, I moved to the threshold. There wasn't a hallway like I expected. Instead, the dead cop lay sprawled on a landing overlooking a den. The decor reminded me of an upscale fishing lodge in the mountains. Antlers and deer heads hung off the oak-paneled walls below. A large tarpon twisted in mid-jump over a gas fireplace.

The thought crossed my mind—who the hell has a fireplace in Florida?

Common sense came to me, reminding me I was still naked. What had they done with my clothes?

A cursory search of the room found me nothing. I paused over the corpse of Twenty-two—Tommy. He wasn't thin, but his frame was definitely smaller than mine. The cop's uniform might fit me, but unlike the regular shirt I stole from Clay earlier, the attire might not blend in as well. Anyone who knew the dead cop would immediately realize I wasn't him.

Still, I picked up his thirty-eight. I might be running naked through the house, but at least I could handle almost anyone that came in.

The door next to the girl's bedroom led to a bathroom, and I grabbed a towel and soaked it under the faucet. Swiftly, I swabbed the blood off my body, careful not to rub the raw wounds. Inside the medicine cabinet, I found two boxes of Band-Aids and some antiseptic cream. After applying some to the bandage pads, I covered the bloody square where I was missing the flesh on my chest with six different bandages. Then I stuck a large Band-Aid over those. After I used all the bandages and left the little paper backings all over the sink, I examined myself in the mirror. Latex bandages covered my scarred tattoo, which, thankfully, remained attached to me. The cuts in my arms from the ropes still showed, but they would have to wait for attention that they so desperately needed.

A door shut downstairs, and I flipped the light off in the bathroom.

"Andy?" a man called from the first floor. "Hurry up."

I held my breath and moved to the door.

"Andy? Tommy?" The newcomer's voice grew louder. "We're waiting outside."

A creak echoed through the house as he made his way up the stairs. If someone was waiting outside, they'd hear any gunshots. How many were there? I had precious little time. As soon as this guy crested the top of the stairs, he'd see the dead cop. Maybe he'd look in the room before he called for help. I had the element of surprise. One step into the hallway, and I'd drop him before he saw the body. But who would come charging to the rescue?

"Shit!" he cursed, having reached the landing.

I let out a belabored moan, loud enough to draw his attention.

"Who's there?" he shouted.

"It's Tommy," I groaned somewhat incoherently. "He shot me."

"Shit!" the man cried again as he shuffled toward the door. "Are you okay?"

His fingers hit the light switch as I swung my fist into his face. The shock and awe factor sent him back, and the nine-millimeter in his hand still pointed at the ground. With a long stride, I rushed him, jabbing the barrel of the thirty-eight into his throat like a battering ram. My left hand whirled around with the butt of the twenty-two pistol, cracking him against the temple.

The figure crashed into the banister, and the wooden railing emitted an audible crack. I smacked him again in the face with the thirty-eight as I hopped back and planted a front kick into his chest. The extra force shattered the barrier, and the man tumbled off the edge into the den below. I neared the edge and peered down. His back landed on a leather couch, but his head hung at an awful angle where it struck the oak coffee table.

I wasn't sure what the record was for killing people in the nude, but I didn't want to break it. I needed clothes.

There was another room past the bathroom, and inside, I found a second bedroom. Either Tommy's or Jace's. When I opened the closet, I assumed it was Jace's. The first shirt I found fit around my broad shoulders. Although it was a little tight, it worked. The shorts were a better fit. His waist was a thirty-six like mine. Unfortunately, when it came to shoes, I was at least two sizes larger than him.

Luckily, the dead cop wore the same size as I did, and I slipped into his boots without socks. Hell would freeze over before I took a dead man's socks.

Now that I had clothes, I pulled two speed loaders off the cop for his thirty-eight. In my back pocket, I placed his retractable baton. Downstairs, I found the nine-millimeter the man in the den dropped during his fall. He carried two magazines in his pants, too. Those slipped into my right pocket.

I peeked out the window of the door. Outside, I saw a couple of ATVs. One was emblazoned with the word "Police" and wrapped in the traditional black and white colors. The other was a bright orange Can-Am Commander. Three men, including another policeman, leaned against the vehicles. Two were talking, mostly with their hands. The cop, though, was looking antsy. He might be wondering where his partner was.

The second thirty-eight revolver was a Smith & Wesson, and I slipped it under my waistband at the small of my back. I slid the twenty-two into my right pocket, and I kept the other thirty-eight in my right hand. With the nine in my left, I took a deep breath before I walked outside to engage the three men.

The ATVs sat parallel to each other and the house. The door pushed open, and I stepped out.

"About time," one of the two talkers blurted out as the door swung open.

He turned to me as my right hand came up. My gun cracked, and I shot the man in the face. Guy number two scrambled away from his now-dead friend as the next bullet struck him in the back of the head.

Before I could turn to him, the cop dove behind the police ATV and started firing at me. The nine-millimeter in my left hand fired rapidly. Its bullets pinged and popped off the ATV's frame, keeping the officer huddled for cover. Without looking, he stuck his gun over the rear cargo area and squeezed off five rounds. I dropped to the ground on the other side of the vehicle. After a few seconds, the gunfire ended. The trees and sky still vibrated with the ringing aftereffects. Lying on the dirt, I aimed the thirty-eight under the ATV, waiting and holding my breath.

Ten seconds passed before the cop's confidence returned. He moved slightly—looking over the top of the ATV's backend. The rear right tire shielded most of his body. When another five seconds ticked past, he stood up slowly. I envisioned him staring down the barrel of a matching thirty-eight. He was wondering if he shot me. His feet shuffled on the gravel, coming from behind the black rubber tire.

The iron sight on the barrel lined up with the man's right shin. I squeezed the trigger. The gun bucked, and the cop dropped into a clump on the ground. I fired again and again. Each time the bullets burrowed into the man, but his feet and ass were pointing at me. I rolled to my feet, keeping both guns up. With two steps, I moved around the back of the ATV.

The officer squirmed on the ground. His right hand extended toward a near identical thirty-eight revolver, just out of reach.

"Don't do it!" I warned.

The cop stared up at me. His face contorted in pain. Blood mixed with the gravel and dirt under him. A lot of blood. I must have hit something vital.

"Roll over," I ordered.

"I can't," he replied weakly.

"You're bleeding to death," I told him. "Let me help you."

"Fuck you," he howled, reaching again for the gun. His movements were slowing.

"Man, you're dying."

"Where's Andy?" he asked as he collapsed onto his back.

"Andy?"

"The other cop?" I responded. "He's dead. So is everyone else in the house."

"Ohh!" he moaned.

"You don't have to die too," I said.

He shook his head. "Too late," he muttered.

Some part of me told me I should feel bad for the guy. He was bleeding out alone in a driveway of a big house that he likely couldn't afford. That same little voice in my head wanted to assume he didn't join the police department to be a bad guy. It wasn't a hard and fast rule, but most bad people didn't start out that way. It was a slow progression. Tiny sacrifices of their morals gave way to bigger choices and harsher consequences.

After all, what really separated this dying policeman and me? It was likely that I'd killed more people than he had. Did that make me a worse person? Or could my justifications turn the tide, making me the good guy? Or did none of it matter? Perhaps the line between good and bad only existed in our minds. That wasn't something I believed, and for the moment, my beliefs were all that mattered.

I turned in a circle, studying the house behind me. If I was at Connors's house, it must not be far from the Quonset huts. Rikki didn't seem to be here.

Was she anywhere? Had Connors hog-tied her too, just to torture information out of her? He'd obviously left the house, thinking Tommy and these guys would operate as guards if I caused any problems.

As I stepped over the dying cop, I kicked the gun away from him before kneeling down.

"Do you know where Connors has the girl?" I asked.

The cop's hand slid to his waist, and I caught it before it wrapped around the hilt of a knife. I slid the blade and sheath off his belt. It wasn't a police issue. The handle was hand-carved from some kind of antler. The stainless-steel blade held a razor-sharp edge. With no manufacturer markings, I thought it might be hand-forged. A script was etched into the steel—*Sinn Féin*.

I touched the point of the blade against the cop's cheek. "The girl?"

He stared up at me with pale, nearly lifeless eyes.

"Where did Connors go?" I asked.

Without answering, the man closed his eyes. He took shallow breaths as his heart slowed.

"Dammit," I mumbled under my breath as I rolled him over.

With the knife, I cut two long strips off the man's shirt and created a tourniquet around his leg. The bleeding was already slow, and it might be too late. I hooked my arms under the cops and lifted him from behind. After dragging him inside, I laid him on the floor, leaning against a column, before moving to the kitchen.

The Connorses kept a well-stocked fridge, and I pulled some orange juice out. I took a glass into the other room and forcibly poured it down his throat. After half of it spilled down his front, I noticed his Adam's apple moving as he swallowed some of it.

A minute later, he'd drunk the rest of the glass and slowly opened his eyes.

"That was a lot of effort," I sighed. "Now, don't die."

He blinked at me, too weak to speak.

"Is Connors going to the other buildings? The huts?" I asked as I took the glass from him and refilled it.

His chin dipped slightly. I took it as a nod.

"I don't know when help will arrive," I told him. "Sip your juice and try not to die."

I stuck the glass in his hand before standing up and heading for the door.

21

The sun was dipping lower, and Gray Connors didn't figure he'd be back before dark. That was okay with him, too. He didn't like the idea of what Carla was doing there. It wasn't that the idea made him overly squeamish, but he hadn't seen this side of his wife in years. She'd adapted to domesticity, seeming to be happy to raise the kids.

When Lily died, Gray worried she would break then. But she hadn't. In fact, it seemed like she got stronger. Or maybe she just focused on the boys more. Jace was her favorite, though. His death cracked her open.

If killing the big guy made her feel better, then it was worth it. He just didn't like seeing her that way.

Connors was certain he wasn't a Fed. He had a Marine tattoo, and if he'd been a cop, he'd have been raising more hell than he did. The man was trying to make a last-ditch effort to save his life. After Carla was done with him, there'd be nothing to find, anyway.

The girl, on the other hand, might have some value. He'd brought a few girls into the States for his contact in the cartel. From what he understood, the market in other countries was even better. Even if she ended up shipped off to some desert country where they kept their wives in chains or whatever they did, she'd be out of Gray's hair. It might even fetch him a nice return.

The Bronco bounced over the rough trail when the handheld radio on the passenger's seat chirped.

"Someone's shooting at the house," a static-laced voice announced.

Gray slammed the brakes, lurching forward. The radio rolled off the seat onto the floor.

He leaned across trying to grab it, but it had bounced out of reach of his fingers.

"Dammit!" he shouted at the top of his lungs. He shifted to neutral and pulled the parking brake up. As soon as he released the buckle on his seatbelt, he stretched the extra few inches to wrap his fingers around the rubber antenna.

"Is someone at the house?" he called over the radio.

"This is Becker. I'm heading there now. Carlton and Andy were on-site."

"Carlton. Andy. Come in." Gray tried not to scream into the radio.

No answer.

"Becker, I'm on my way back," Connor informed the man on the other end. "Secure the house and call me back."

Gray dropped the radio onto the seat again as he released the brake. The Bronco jerked back as he reversed into the woods.

The house was three miles back. Even though these trails were clear, it would still take him ten minutes to follow the switchbacks winding through the woods.

The drive felt like an eternity. He picked up the radio twice, thinking about calling Becker for an update.

No, he warned himself. The man would call when he could. Better to maintain radio silence.

When the Bronco came out of the forest into the clearing, Gray pointed it across the pasture to the house on the other side of the property. His tires flung gravel up as the Bronco fishtailed onto the rocky drive that bordered his property.

Behind him, powder-white dust hung in the air as the little sport utility vehicle stirred up the dry gravel. When he slammed on the brakes, the tires slid to a stop with a long crunch.

In front of the house was the Como Police Departments ATV. An unmistakable bloodstain mixed with the limestone rocks. Connors stalked around the vehicle, pausing in his tracks over the two bodies. Tim Wilson and his brother—what was his name?—Jeffrey. Both men were shot dead. Head shots. Tim stretched out on his back. His face was a mess of cartilage, bone, and flesh. Even dental records would prove difficult in identifying the man. The gunshot obliterated his face. Jeffrey was face down in the dirt, thankfully. The back of his head ripped open.

"Carla!" Gray shouted, rotating on his left heel before running into the house.

Becker knelt in the den next to a body. Carlton. He was Ledoux's partner.

"Is he—"

"He's alive," Becker told him. "Barely. Looks like someone dragged him inside and saved his life."

"Carla?"

Becker glanced up at Gray without a word. The older man ran up the stairs.

"Shit!" he cursed as he reached the landing and Andy Ledoux's body. Through the door of Lily's room, he had a clear view of his wife. Sticky, brown blood caked the carpeted floor.

Gray Connors stepped over the officer's corpse and into his daughter's room. His stomach roiled, and bile filled his throat. He turned his head and vomited away from his dead wife. Heaving the contents of his stomach over the floor, he collapsed to his knees.

"I'm so sorry, Carla," he apologized. "I didn't mean to mess everything up."

Connors smeared the dribbles of vomit from his chin with the back of his hand as he crawled to his wife. As he pulled her into his arms, he stared under the table at the figure of Tommy lying on his back, the black power cord draped across his chest like a bolo tie.

Gray Connors felt the rage inside him burning up. He pulled his wife's face close to his and kissed her cheek.

"Becker!" he called downstairs.

Footsteps sounded on the stairs as the tall man stepped over the police officer.

"Give me your radio!"

Becker unclipped the walkie-talkie from his belt and handed it gingerly to the man cradling his deceased wife.

Gray clicked the call button. "Alex and Drew, come in!"

"Go ahead," Alex replied.

"Secure the girl. The guy is loose. I want everyone out after him."

"Roger that," Alex responded.

Gray continued, "You put someone with a gun against that bitch's head. If he shows up, blow the whore away."

"I wouldn't do that if I were you," a voice came through the radio.

Gray growled into the mic. "I gave you an order. If you don't do it, I'll come take care of her myself. You too!"

"I've got it, sir," Alex told him. "That wasn't me."

"I'm warning you not to do it," the voice came through again.

"It's you!" Gray shouted. "You fucking killed my wife and son!"

"Connors, I told you earlier it was on you."

"I'll kill you myself, you bastard!"

"At this point, you don't have much more to lose, do you?"

"Who the fuck do you think you are?" Connors screamed into the radio.

"I'm a fucking Marine, asshole. To anyone that's still listening—Drew or Alex or whoever—this is your one warning. If anything happens to the girl, I'll kill every one of you. When I'm done, this little shithole community will be wiped off the map. I'd run if I was you."

"Dammit!" Gray screamed into the radio, letting Carla slide to the floor as he stood up.

He marched out of his daughter's room and down the stairs. The weak eyes of the police officer stared at him. This asshole bandaged up the cop but left Carla upstairs to bleed to death. He strangled Tommy. Gray pulled a forty-five-caliber H&K from his belt and shot Carlton the cop in the head.

"Mr. Connors!" Becker exclaimed.

"If they didn't deserve to be saved, then neither did he," Connors stated. "You tell everyone, if they try to run from this asshole, I'll be the one to kill them myself. Them and their families. I don't give a shit anymore."

He stormed out of the house and climbed into the Bronco. When the door slammed shut, he picked up his radio.

"Marine, if you want the bitch alive, you'll come get her."

The radio remained silent. Did he turn it off?

"Roger," a voice replied through the static.

22

She'd been balled up in the fetal position for hours. Rikki lost track of time a while back. All she knew was it cramped everything on her. Each attempt to move a leg or an arm scraped against the metal bars of the dog cage.

The assholes put her in a dog cage. Not even a big one that could handle a Doberman or German shepherd. There was enough room for her to keep her knees in her chest—that was about it.

Besides forcing her into the kennel, no one had hurt her. Yet.

That asshole who grabbed her at the door made sure she knew what was going to happen to her. If Chase hadn't shown up right then, he might have followed through with his threat. Instead, he had someone force her into the cage and keep a gun on her. At least for a bit.

Outside, it sounded like a war zone. Chase was fucking these guys up, she thought. Every second, she expected him to burst through the door. Of course, that was almost ridiculous. Even Chase was outgunned out there. He hadn't come here on a rescue mission—that much was obvious.

No, Rikki considered. He came in to scout the place, and when he saw Rikki with the blond kid, everything went to hell.

She wanted to kick herself. Had she just stayed away, things might have turned out differently.

Especially after she heard the one they called Drew say they got him. What did that mean—"got him"? Was Chase dead?

When Drew stopped hovering over her, she worried it was true. Now, they thought she no longer needed an armed guard standing over her. That could only mean one thing—Chase wasn't a problem anymore. Until then, she assumed she was bait or a last-ditch defense for him. If he showed up and Drew held a gun to her head, how much damage could he do? Now, though, they didn't seem concerned with her.

Every so often, she thrashed with all her might against the cage. The metal rocked and rattled, but in her position, she couldn't get the leverage to bend the bars. Between those attempts, she remained still, frustrated, and lost in her thoughts.

At some point, someone was going to take her out of this prison. She needed to act. Her only task now was to figure out how to get out of here.

Several hours went by, and the energy in the building changed. Drew reappeared, but he moved with visible agitation. He had another guy with him.

"Hey!" she shouted. "I need to go to the bathroom."

"Shut up!" Drew yelled, kicking the cage. The blow rocked her in her little wire box.

"Do what he said," the other man ordered.

Drew pulled a Glock nine-millimeter handgun out and leveled it between the bars.

"What the hell?" Rikki exclaimed.

"At this point, you don't have much more to lose, do you?" a voice came over the other guy's radio. It was Chase.

A gravelly voice sounded through the radio. "Who the fuck do you think you are?"

Chase responded, "I'm a fucking Marine, asshole. To anyone that's still listening—Drew or Alex or whoever—this is your one warning. If anything happens to the girl, I'll kill everyone of you. When I'm done, this little shithole community will be wiped off the map. I'd run if I was you."

The two men glanced at each other nervously.

"What do we do?" the second man asked Drew as he turned the volume down on the walkie-talkie.

Rikki's face broke into a big smile. "If I were you, I'd let me out before he gets here."

"No way that happens," Drew snapped. "I don't want to go up against Gray."

Rikki snorted. "Have you ever pissed off a Marine?"

The two men scowled at her.

"He's not just any Marine," Rikki told them. "He's the guy they sent in to kill everyone."

"That's bullshit," Drew retorted.

"He was Recon—that's Special Forces. He'll cut a path right up to the door."

"No, no, no," Drew stammered, shaking his head. "Gray will kill our families if we cross him."

"I don't know, Drew," the other guy argued. "Did you see what this guy did before they got him?"

"Yeah, Alex, but Tommy caught him."

"Obviously not," Alex pointed out. "He's out there threatening Gray now. Hell, he called us by name."

"We hold her here until they say differently," Drew explained. "If this Marine makes it here, we'll figure it out."

"Your funeral," Rikki said flatly.

Drew kicked the cage again. Somewhere in another part of the building, a phone rang. Alex gave Drew a hard look.

"Go answer it," Drew ordered him.

Alex vanished from the room.

"Can't you, at least, let me out?" Rikki asked. "I need to use the bathroom."

"Shut up!" Drew ordered as Alex returned.

"Gray wants us to stay off the radios," he told Drew. "And he wants her moved."

Drew nodded to the other guy, motioning for him to unlock the cage.

"If you do anything, I'll shoot you," he warned her.

When the gate opened, Rikki squirmed around until she could back out slowly. Her legs had gone numb, and when she attempted to stand up, she wobbled. Alex grabbed her arm, directing her through the door where he'd just come from. As soon as his fingers wrapped around her upper arm, Rikki twisted, catching Alex by the wrist and throwing him to the ground.

Drew took two strides forward as he reeled back his hand. The side of the Glock struck her against the head, and Rikki's knees buckled under her. She caught the door frame as she settled into a kneel.

"Don't try that again!" Drew demanded. "Next time I'll kill you."

"You won't have a human shield then," Rikki mumbled somewhat incoherently.

Alex pushed up off the floor. "Sorry, I didn't expect that," he muttered.

"Get her up," Drew countered. "Don't let her do it again."

Alex nodded bashfully.

"Where are we going?" Rikki asked once she got back to her feet. She touched the side of her head, feeling the gash left by the steel of the nine-millimeter. A line of blood slipped from her temple and ran down her cheek. Her right index and middle finger wiped it away, leaving a smear across her face. As she passed through the door, she strafed the bloody fingers along the drywall in a smeared trail.

"Doesn't matter," Drew stated.

Rikki marched through a corridor to a large warehouse. Pallets with large wooden boxes were stacked in rows along the floor. Drew and Alex prodded her between the lines of crates toward an open overhead door. As she walked, her eyes scanned for an opening to escape, although the two men stayed just close enough to shoot her if she tried.

Somehow, Rikki suspected they didn't intend to kill her yet. This Gray person, who Alex and Drew feared, sounded angry with Chase. She figured either she was going to be bait or some sort of incentive. Or she might be just a hostage to slow Chase down. That seemed like a mistake. Rikki knew Chase. He would not assume that because someone said they wouldn't kill her, that it would be true. He would not stop, even if they threatened to kill her. She didn't blame him either. Her only hope was escape, either on her own or with Chase. These people thought by using her they could slow him down.

No, Chase might back off for a second, but that would only be to get a running start. And she didn't expect this Gray would not kill her. If he eluded Chase, then Rikki would be of no use to him.

When she stepped into the night air, she paused. Forty men surrounded the front of the building. The atmosphere felt charged with anxiety and fear. What the hell had Chase done to get them this nervous?

A grin crept over her face as she thought about how one man scared an entire army.

"Get her in the car!" Drew ordered a guy lingering in the back. "Everyone else, be on alert. This guy is coming here for her."

There was a murmuring that crossed through the men like a wave. Rikki glanced back at the gathering as this new guy ushered her toward a black GMC Yukon. The forest cracked with a gunshot. Rikki didn't see who got hit, but the throng of men scattered away in panic. The door jerked open as she was shoved into the back seat. She turned to see two men in the front seat. Drew and Alex jumped into the backseat on either side of her, pushing her to the center.

"Get out of here!" Drew shouted, slamming the door.

The driver pulled the gearshift into drive and hit the gas. Rikki glanced over her shoulder at the mayhem out there.

"He's in the woods," Alex announced.

The driver's window shattered, and he jerked the wheel to the right, sending the back of the Yukon around.

"Is he shooting at us?" the passenger asked.

"Yeah," the driver responded, keeping his focus ahead of him.

The SUV raced through the gates as the window on the rear right quarter exploded. Rikki ducked her head into her lap. She trusted Chase would not shoot her intentionally, but even a stray bullet or flying piece of glass could slip through.

"Doesn't he know she's in here?" Alex questioned.

With her face in her knees, Rikki replied, "Oh, he knows."

"I thought he wanted to save you?" he asked.

"Didn't you hear him over the radio, Alex?" Rikki mumbled. "He told you to run away."

"Shit!" the passenger exclaimed. "He's going to kill us all."

"Floor it!" Drew ordered, ducking his head too.

The driver whipped the wide GMC truck along the tight curves of the trail designed for smaller ATVs. He braked, letting the rear of the Yukon go into a skid that tapped a tree with a slight crunch before he gunned the motor, racing away.

"There's something following us," the passenger alerted the driver.

"I know," was the only response.

Rikki lifted her head and turned back to see bright headlights racing up on the back of the Yukon.

"He can outrun us," the driver informed the others.

Drew rolled his window down before sticking his torso out of the opening. His Glock flashed as he fired back at the pursuing vehicle.

"Help him," the driver urged the passenger and Alex.

The guy in the passenger seat stuck his arm out the window and started firing. Rikki couldn't make out the gun, while she kept her head down, praying Chase could handle them.

"Alex, shoot the asshole!" the driver shouted.

"I can't," he mumbled.

Rikki turned to glance up at Drew, who leaned farther out the window. He paused to reload, and Rikki sat up swiftly, rotated toward him, and threw her shoulder into the man. Alex caught her by the arm, pulling her back as Drew lost his balance, tumbling out of the Yukon.

"What the fuck!" the passenger shouted, pointing his Smith & Wesson forty-four at her face.

"Gray wants her alive," Alex interjected.

"Fuck Gray, let's toss her out," the passenger said.

"Shut up, Jimmy," the driver ordered. He let out a sigh. "There, we have company now."

The other two men turned to look back as four more headlights raced toward the ATV, following them. Rikki stared over the seat through the back window as the lights converged on the vehicle Chase was driving. Suddenly the three ATVs collided, or, at least, it looked like it from the conglomeration of lights that now slowed as the Yukon pulled away.

"What about Drew?" Alex asked.

"He might be okay," the driver told him.

The lights behind them disappeared as the SUV rounded a curve in the trail. Rikki watched out the back, waiting for Chase to show back up. Minutes passed, and the forest behind them remained dark.

He could be running with no lights, she thought.

Then the trees were gone, and they drove out onto a field. No, not a field. It was an airstrip.

The Yukon pulled up next to an Aerostar airplane. The door jerked open, and a graying man stared at her. "Get her out," he ordered the other three. "Where's Drew?"

Alex answered, "She pushed him out the window."

The man turned to stare at her. His eyes burned with an empty glare. It was as if whatever had been behind them vanished.

"Put her on the plane."

"The guy was chasing us, but I think our guys stopped him."

The angry man grunted, "Get her aboard. We leave in two minutes."

23

The first Polaris barreled into the Can-Am with a thunderous crash that shook the ground like an earthquake. I had barely enough time to turn my vehicle right before it happened, but the impact still sent me careening off the trail and over a log. My back end crashed down hard with an earsplitting snap that seemed to stop the clock as the engine screamed in protest, trying so desperately to move the immovable weight of my Can-Am.

My hand grabbed the 30-06 I'd taken off one of the men outside the compound, and I scrambled out of the ATV and into the ditch at the side of the road. The other two Polaris ATVs made a sharp U-turn. Multiple headlight beams illuminated the trees around me. Before I could hit the ground, bullets started plowing up dirt around me as the occupants of those two vehicles opened fire on the Can-Am. I rolled down the opposite embankment, hoping to find safety in the dark.

"He's out!" someone called.

My feet scrambled away into the shadows.

"Get after him!"

The air shuddered with the sound of gunfire. I ducked instinctively as rounds whizzed past me, shards of stone and bark raining onto the ground like a torrential downpour. My only consolation for the moment was that these guys didn't know quite where I was. Of course, none of that stopped blind luck from putting a stray bullet through my head.

If I didn't do something to even up the odds, they'd outgun me, eventually. Sprawled on the ground, I peered back toward the gunfire.

The lights from the ATVs shone in my eyes, menacingly bright and blinding me with their searing glow, just as they had done the night before. With one eye closed, I stared down the barrel of the rifle, taking aim at where I knew the driver would be sitting. I squeezed the trigger of the 30-06 and braced as the gun kicked against my shoulder.

"Dammit!" came an agonized cry from within the car. "He hit me!"

"Scatter!" Another man shouted, but his words were met with a desperate plea.

"Wait," begged the driver who I'd just shot. "I can't."

My blood boiled as I loosened my grip on the rifle. Adrenaline coursed through me—a byproduct of battle.

With a slow, deep breath, I slipped the rifle's shoulder strap over my arm and let it hang off my back. The rush of a firefight couldn't rule my decisions. That carnal side of my brain reminded me that once I knew where he was, I could take another shot. A killing shot.

But that seemed somewhat unsportsmanlike. A kill for no reason. Right now, he couldn't hurt me, and as far as I was concerned, that took him off the table.

Besides, I had at least two or three uninjured men now in the woods looking for me.

My right hand pulled the Glock nine-millimeter up. It was going to be a little more useful in the close combat. Cold steel in my hand reassured me as I crept through the blackness of the forest, taking care to stay out of the beams of the headlights that flooded the trees and in the oppressive and murky darkness beyond.

The human eye worked wonders, and mine were working overtime as they tried to adapt. Unfortunately, the bright lumens of the LEDs engulfing the trees disrupted any adjustment my vision might make to the dark. I knew it would be just as difficult for the others to maneuver in that kind of environment as it was for me, so I steeled myself and stepped into the shadows.

I gritted my teeth and crouched down, lowering my frame closer to the ground. My mind was racing, partly because I had no way of knowing how much time I had to save Rikki before her situation became even more desperate.

What could be worse than this?

At least for now, I was safe from the clutches of a deranged mother. Memories of a mad woman slicing at my skin with a wicked blade rushed at me, but I pushed them away with a shudder. There was no time to think about that now—I had to act quickly before it was too late.

Besides, they all feared me. Word spread quickly in the ranks—I was paramount to the boogeyman. I saw it in their reaction at the compound. Thirty or more men trembled at the thought of little old me out in the woods hunting them.

An animal was making a sharp, high-pitched chittering in the tree above my head. A few seconds later, I heard the hoot of an owl. The sound exploded into the night air and ricocheted off the surrounding walls. Then the leaves crunched just outside my position, like someone or something was walking through them. Popping up like a jack-in-the-box, I twisted around and fired a single shot into a figure that was only a few yards away. As he fell to the ground, I was already moving deeper into the forest with perfect silence as my ally. His buddies opened fire on my location while I ran through the trees, staying just out of their line of sight. As the gunfire masked any other sounds, I wasted no time moving through the darkness to flank them.

"Stop firing!" one of them hollered. The volley ended.

"Who's hit?" someone asked. I tracked the voice through the dark until I made out a faint silhouette.

"I'm good."

"Shut up!" another person shouted.

I lined up the sights of the Glock and took aim at the shape in the distance. My finger hesitated on the trigger for a split second, then I squeezed it, feeling the gun buck as the figure crumpled to the ground.

"Dammit!"

"Jason, wait!"

A man ran back to one of the Polaris ATVs, jumping in the driver's seat.

"Wait!" the voice called again, and I realized it was the driver I'd shot in the other vehicle.

Jason didn't stick around, though. The Polaris screamed to life and made a quick turnaround before speeding back into the woods. I didn't move, watching for any other movement. I'd dropped two in the dark and shot the driver. Was there anyone else out here in the woods?

I stayed crouched for a moment, the silence pressing in like fog. The faint groan of the driver pierced my ears, and I slowly stood, Glock tense in my grip. Every breath seemed to echo in my head as I moved around the back of the Polaris. My eyes found the driver huffing for a breath.

Slumped back in his seat, the man's head leaned back against the headrest. Blood soaked through the fabric of his shirt and pooled on the floor of the cab. When I looked at it closely, I saw a ragged wound seeping blood slowly from his chest. He was pale and painfully still. I knew that even if I raced him to the hospital now, his odds of survival were slim.

"He left me," the man complained.

"You can't really get good help nowadays," I remarked, studying him.

"I'm not going to make it," he wheezed.

I shook my head, reaching across and taking a Smith & Wesson thirty-eight from beside him. "If you had a chopper, they might get you to a hospital in time."

"You could finish me," he suggested.

My head cocked to the side. "No, I don't think I can."

"Give me the gun, then," he pleaded.

"Again, I don't think I can."

"Shit," he murmured. "I'm sorry."

Ignoring his trite apology, I asked, "Where were they taking the girl?"

"The airstrip."

"Damn!" I cursed. "Where is it?"

"North of here," he said. "Please give me the gun. Let me end it."

I reached over and grabbed him by the arm. "Tell you what," I offered as I heaved him over into the passenger's seat. "Let's get you to the airstrip. Either someone will shoot you or maybe they'll get you some help."

"It won't matter," he reiterated.

"Best deal I can offer you, though."

He didn't respond. I left him for a second, wandering in the dark until I found the two men I'd shot. Both were dead. I rifled through their pockets until I came out with extra ammo—three magazines for the Glock.

When I turned the key of my Polaris ATV, a sudden jolt of vibration rumbled up from the engine. The injured man moaned, his eyes fluttering open, as I eased the vehicle into reverse and headed back along the narrow dirt trail.

"That way?" I asked.

He nodded.

As I drove north toward the airfield, dread filled the empty spaces in my gut. If Connors took off with Rikki in tow, I would run short of options. But I knew that if there was information to be found, I would do whatever it took to get it. Despite the fear of facing unknown consequences, I kept pushing forward, determined to find out what was waiting for me.

When I pulled out of the woods, I saw four sets of headlights gleaming down the grassy runway. Fifty yards away, two airplanes sat at the end of the airstrip—a twin engine Aerostar and a smaller Cessna. The windows in the Aerostar glowed from the interior lights, and the door still hung open, casting a rectangular light on the ground. A figure jogged to the plane, climbing up the steps into the bright opening.

Gray Connors was easily recognizable. He froze in the opening, staring out at me. Or at least the Polaris that just arrived on the scene. His right index finger lifted toward me, and I could see the man shouting an order. Then he stepped inside and pulled the hatch closed.

I guessed Rikki was on the plane, and if I didn't stop them, they'd be off the ground in a minute.

As I revved the engine, one of the other ATVs pulled out of formation, heading my direction. The other two remained with their lights directed down the grassy airstrip. They couldn't move until the plane took off, since they were acting as runway lights.

The guy beside me groaned as I raced over the field. If I could block the plane's path, they'd have a hard time taking off. The Aerostar began moving as the ATV made a suicide run at me. My Glock came up, and I fired at the lights. At this distance, while not only moving but also driving, my aim was shit. I knew I wasn't hitting the mark, and the vehicle flew toward me.

With no choice, I jerked the wheel away from the runway, making a wide arc in the other direction. The Glock switched from my right hand to my left. I opened fire again as I came around.

A loud pop sounded—like a tire blowing. Headlights on the other vehicle veered toward me for a split second before the ATV came to a jarring stop.

With an increased whirring sound, the Aerostar began picking up speed, and I floored the accelerator. My Polaris jumped and bounced over the field as I tried to catch up to the aircraft. It continued picking up speed, but I was gaining on it. Just not fast enough. The plane was running out of grass as the trees ahead grew taller.

I was within a hundred feet of the plane when the wheels lifted off the runway. I raised the Glock to fire but paused. If I hit something vital, it might not affect them until they were high enough to cause a crash. Rikki would be in danger then. As if she wasn't in enough trouble already.

As the aircraft rose in the air, I continued up underneath it, unable to stop its takeoff or get aboard it. I braked, taking the Polaris into a skid.

The dying man next to me slumped over. I started to reach for him when I saw the other two ATVs running full speed toward me.

24

A volley of bullets pecked at the front of the Polaris. The plastic windshield peppered with cracks. I spun the wheel to the left. The guy next to me slid lifelessly off the edge. I thought I'd lost him. If I hadn't been trying to evade gunfire, I might have felt a bit of sympathy for the man.

These idiots stayed on my tail, firing at the rear of my ATV as I fishtailed around. My only plan was to make it harder for them to get a target. But I was running out of runway too. The forest loomed ahead, and I didn't want to dive into the trees again. I'd enjoyed all the leaves and sticks and dirt I could stand.

My foot hit the brake as I turned the wheel. The back tires slid in the grass, tearing up swaths of green under the rubber as I made a 180-degree turn. My pursuers were close enough behind me that once I was all the way around, they had a split second before we passed each other.

In the driver's side mirror, I watched the two ATVs turn around. During those few seconds, I put nearly a hundred yards between us. I eyed the Cessna at the other end of the runway.

As a kid in Arkansas, I often spent time with my uncle, who flew crop dusters down in the rice belt. Uncle Charlie taught me how to fly those little planes. He'd never let me land, and I never bothered to get my pilot's license. But I could probably take off—assuming I had a clear runway with no one shooting at me.

I'd never get aboard and start the thing with these guys on my ass. The wheel cut to the right again, aiming the front at the tree line. Reaching back, I pulled the 30-06 around and off my shoulder. The front of the ATV aimed at a wide opening in the woods where the trail started. I jammed the rifle through the wheel and against the accelerator. As we zoomed toward the trees, I cut off the lights, plunging myself and the Polaris into darkness.

As the ATV roared through the darkness, I dove off the side, hitting the grass on my back and rolling away from the ATV. The Polaris continued toward the forest, and ten seconds later, the other two ATVs raced past me. Luckily, they were far enough from me to neither see me nor, more importantly, run over me.

I sprang up after they passed and ran after the two ATVs. Ahead of me, the Polaris wrecked into the trees with a deep crunch. In the dark, I couldn't admire my handiwork. If things worked out, the damned thing would roll over a few times. The other two vehicles came to a stop, and the engine noise halted.

"What did he hit?"

"Hell if I know," another responded. "Let's find him. Hopefully, the crash killed him."

I ran up behind the two. "It didn't," I exclaimed, raising the Glock and firing twice.

Both men fell—although neither shot should kill them. I very much wanted them alive.

The driver of the second ATV turned to fire at me. Before he made it around with his gun, I struck him in the shoulder. When the bullet knocked him around, he twisted like a top. As I ran around the vehicle, I leveled the Glock at his passenger, who tossed his gun into the dark and lifted his hands.

"You guys have a chance to walk away from all this," I pointed out. "I just want some answers."

"C'mon man, please don't kill us," the driver of the first vehicle moaned.

"Answers." My voice harshened as I repeated my demands. Almost collectively, they nodded.

"Where is Connors taking the girl?" I asked.

Three of them offered various head shakes and "I don't know." The second driver, though, said, "He told the pilot 'Mexico.' A town called Las Higerellas or something like that."

"What's there?"

"I don't know. It's above my pay grade."

"What's he bringing in? Can you tell me that?"

"Yeah," the man nodded. "Heroin. A little coke, but mostly heroin."

"Think it's from Mexico."

The passenger in the first ATV responded, "It's definitely from Mexico. Or somewhere that they speak Spanish."

"You." I pointed to the one man I hadn't shot yet. "I want everyone's phones and radios."

"Are you going to kill us?" he asked warily.

"Not if you do this right. Make sure one phone is unlocked—permanently."

He nodded and pulled his own phone out. The screen glowed against his face as he did something on it. Then he collected the other three cellphones and four walkie-talkies.

"Listen up. Connors is never coming back here. Whatever you do next is up to you. I am taking this ATV," I told them, pointing at the closest one. "You guys better take the other and race back to get medical help. If you follow me, I'll just kill you all."

I received a round of affirmatives and nods.

I climbed into the ATV and turned the engine over until it started. The Glock resting across the wheel as I backed it up.

When I reached the plane, I pulled the chocks from around the wheels. Once I got in the cockpit, I wasn't wasting time. There wouldn't be much of a preflight checklist. Especially since I didn't really have any idea what I should be checking. Charlie never covered that part with me. Plus, I expected more men might be on their way. If that was the case, I wanted the engine running and my takeoff started before anyone got in my way.

I scrambled through the cockpit and found the keys in the ignition. A smile slid across my face. This was, after all, out in the country. Of course, Connors left the key. It saved me time. Otherwise, I was going to have to hot-wire it—something I'd never done before.

The Lycoming engine turned over several times before firing. As it rumbled, I checked the fuel gauge. It was only sitting at about a quarter of a tank. Not enough to go far, but hopefully sufficient for getting out of here. The other gauges—temperature and oil pressure—looked good. Although Uncle Charlie's plane was a lot simpler than this one, I thought I understood what I was supposed to be looking at. Everything was in the green, or, at least, it wasn't in the red.

There were several steps to taking off, and I hadn't done it in years. The last few times I'd flown, I took over after takeoff.

One thing I was positive about was I needed to give the engine gas. Small planes like this, and perhaps even big jets as far as I knew, had a control for mixing the richness of the fuel. Again, Charlie glossed over this part of my lesson, so I had no real idea what that entailed, only that it was important.

I pushed the fuel mixture knob all the way in. There was no way I'd be able to figure out the proper amount. What I remembered was not to pull it all the way out or the engine would stall. That seemed an important fact even when I was a kid.

Once the engine started humming faster, I found the black throttle knob and pushed it forward as well. The plane began rolling forward.

Out the cockpit window I saw the headlights of the other ATV turn around before heading off into the woods.

The Cessna picked up speed. I couldn't see anything outside the window except the reflection on the inside of the instrument panel. The throttle was all the way in, and I prayed I reached takeoff speed before I reached the tree line.

The airspeed climbed past thirty knots.

Forty.

Forty-five.

The plane bounced across the field. It might have looked like a flat piece of ground, but it was far from as smooth as asphalt.

Fifty knots.

Fifty-five. I pulled back on the yoke gently, trying to peer out the window for the tops of the trees.

The nose of the aircraft lifted at about twenty degrees. I continued to pull back, hoping to get into a steeper climb. The airspeed indicator said we were at sixty-five knots. Something scraped the belly of the plane, and I winced, almost closing my eyes—as if keeping them opened mattered when I couldn't see.

Based on the altimeter, the plane continued to climb. Again, that felt like a win. At 1500 feet, I leveled off. The fuel gauge dipped some during takeoff, and I had no idea how to adjust the fuel mixture to save gas. I needed to find a place to put down, and the sooner I did that, the better it would be.

I grabbed the phone I forced the guy to unlock and opened it. I dialed a number for Sam Cornell's cellphone. It was after midnight—in fact, close to two in the morning.

"Hello," Sam answered, sounding fully awake.

"It's Chase."

"Chase, where have you been? You were supposed to check in with me."

"Lots of problems."

"I called the state police this evening," he informed me. "I hadn't heard anything at all. After talking with Benjamin, he agreed it had been too long."

"Sam—"

"Did you find Rikki?"

"Yes," I answered. "But I lost her again. She's on a private plane heading to some place in Mexico. I think it's something like Higerellos or Higerellis. I'm not sure."

"Is she safe?" Sam questioned.

"Not likely," I admitted. "Her foray up the river put her in the middle of a drug-smuggling operation. The guy in charge is named Gray Connors. Right now, he had her on his plane. My guess is he's using her as a hostage to slow me down."

"What do you need?" Sam asked.

"I'm flying a Cessna with almost no fuel. I need a place to put it down safely."

"Where are you?"

I found the GPS and read him the coordinates. "Right now, I'm heading west. If I have no other place to go, I'd just as soon make a water landing."

"Got it," he acknowledged. "There are not a lot of places around there. The closest is an airfield in Steinhatchee."

I pulled up the name of the town on the GPS. "I'm not sure how much fuel I'll need, but I'm changing my heading."

"Stay on the coastline," Sam suggested. "At least if you have to make an emergency landing, the sea will be right there."

"Next, I need a plane."

"Uh—"

"One that can take me to Mexico," I explained. "With an actual pilot."

"Are you not a pilot?" Sam asked.

"No, I'm literally winging this."

"Son of a bitch," the man cursed in his Irish brogue.

"I can handle flying. Landing might be an issue."

"Son of a bitch," Sam repeated.

"Just find me a plane. I'll call back in ten minutes."

After disconnecting with Sam, I dialed another number. The phone rang twice before a deep, almost angry-sounding voice answered with a thick Cuban accent. "Hola."

"Esteban," I greeted the man on the other end of the phone.

"Gordon," he responded flatly. The man on the other end, whose name was Esteban Velasquez, earned the nickname Scar thanks to the jagged scar across his face. Although I never called him that to his face. After all, most people knew the number-one hitter for Julio Moreno, the biggest drug lord in Florida. Moreno and I have had a few run-ins, all of which I've left alive, which led me to think there was a mutual understanding. I wouldn't trust that too far, though.

"You do realize the time?" the man asked.

"Yes, I'm sorry. I need an answer to a quick question."

"Of course," he remarked sarcastically. "I've been waiting up to help any fucking gringo that calls."

"Someone is smuggling heroin into Florida from Mexico. I'm assuming it isn't Julio."

"Mr. Moreno is a businessman."

"Right," I replied, holding back on the sarcasm. "Do you know who would be shipping it in? I think it's coming from someplace called Higerellos. I'm not sure about the name."

"I'll call you back," he said before hanging up.

With a shrug, I dropped the phone onto the console next to the pilot's seat. Both hands grabbed the yoke, and I guided the aircraft north. The phone rang, and I snatched it up.

"Chase," Sam said. "I've got a plane heading to the airstrip. It took some doing, but it will be there in about an hour. What's your ETA?"

"I think about fifteen minutes," I told him.

As soon as I said it, a red light began strobing on the console. Before I could read the gauge, a loud clunk sounded from the motor. The entire aircraft vibrated for two seconds. All the shaking stopped when the motor died. Suddenly, the only thing I could hear was the air racing over the hull.

25

"I got a problem, Sam," I blurted into the phone. "The engine just died."

"What's your coordinates?"

I read out the longitude and latitude to him before dropping the phone onto the console.

"Mayday! Mayday! Mayday!" I called into the radio.

"This is—" the radio chirped before cutting out.

"Come back," I called into the radio.

I got no response. I realized the GPS now showed a black screen. All the console lights went dark. The cockpit had no power.

I let out a string of curse words. With no GPS, I didn't know where to go.

Go west. That was the smartest thing I thought of. Just like I'd told Sam, if I had to crash, the water seemed like a better place to do it.

The principle behind flying seemed similar to that of boating. On a boat, the number one rule was to keep the ocean out of the boat. It made sense that the number one rule in flying should be to keep the plane in the air. Without an engine, that made the task a tad more difficult.

However, I hoped my understanding of aerodynamics was correct. As long as the air provided lift under the wings, I could at the very least slow my descent. In a sailboat, the concept worked the same. Use the sails to catch the wind to provide lift. The only difference was that the sailboat moved horizontally instead of vertically.

I pulled back on the yoke and adjusted the flaps slightly. The nose angled up a bit, and I took advantage of the added lift to veer toward the sea. Right now, the only instruments working were the compass, a traditional old-school needle type, and the altimeter. At least I'd know which direction I flew. The only real problem was the cockpit remained almost pitch black. Luckily, both the compass and the altimeter were equipped with some photo-luminescent indicators allowing them to glow in the dark.

The altimeter read 1000 feet. I continued to pull back on the yoke, keeping the plane on a slow glide out to sea. Once the belly of the plane touched the water, the friction should slow me down. The danger lay in the entire aircraft flipping in the process.

Without any lighting in the cabin, I saw the reflection on the waves below. I tried not to look again. Instead, I focused on the altitude.

Eight hundred feet. The airspeed decreased rapidly too, but the gauge remained useless in the dark. I needed it to slow even more if I didn't want the first impact with the sea to tear the bottom of the plane off or worse. I adjusted the flaps more, pushing the nose toward the stars slightly.

Six hundred fifty feet.

The altitude dropped quickly.

Five hundred seventy-five.

Five hundred.

The surface of the Gulf of Mexico became clearer now. On the horizon, I saw lights on shrimping boats strafing the waters for their nocturnal prey.

Three hundred fifty feet. I pulled back more. The plane didn't respond as easily now.

I stopped checking the altimeter, focusing on the water ahead of me.

Keep it flat, Gordon.

The water appeared to be calm, and I would have smiled if I hadn't been intently heaving back on the yoke. With my right hand, I made a quick final adjustment to the flaps, pulling them all the way back.

First contact with the water sent me reeling forward. Restrained by my seat belt, I recovered as the second impact drove the nose of the plane under the surface. Seawater rushed over the windshield, plunging me into darkness for a minute before the plane regained its buoyancy. The cockpit popped up out of the water.

I leaned back in my seat and let out a deep breath. Instinctively, I reached for the phone, but I couldn't find it. The crash landing likely threw it across the cabin.

So far in my life, I'd never been in a disaster at sea. I'd seen a few. Even rescued someone from a plane crash in the middle of the ocean, but I hadn't been on the other end of it.

In sailing, the safest course of action when one's boat was capsized or otherwise incapacitated was to stay with the boat. It was a much larger object, making it easier to find by rescuers. While I'd yet to have that happen on *Carina*, I did keep a go-bag ready to throw into a lifeboat in an emergency. Now, I didn't have that, but I hoped the plane came with a lifeboat.

My fingers released the restraint, and I scrambled over the seat into the rear cabin. The Cessna held four people comfortably, with two in the cockpit and two in the cabin. Behind the rear seat was the cargo area—where I hoped to find a lifeboat or, barring that, a life vest.

After climbing into the cargo area, I struggled to see anything. The small porthole windows provided limited light in the daytime, but at night with no power, they were pointless. My hands searched around in the dark for anything, pulling a fire extinguisher out from under the rear seat and tossed it forward. Right now, I didn't need it, but at least it would be handy.

In the back, I found a square canvas bag. Immediately, I thought it felt like a deflated raft. It had the ridges made when the rubber was completely devoid of air and folded tightly. Still strapped to the back wall, the raft had never been used. It took a few minutes to remove it.

When I climbed forward again, I unzipped the canvas and pulled out the raft. If I strained my eyes, I could read the label stating the manufacturer had designed it for six people. I ran my fingers over it until I found the pull cord that activated the CO_2 cartridge. Once I pulled it, the raft would fill with air, expanding to full size.

Not something I wanted to do in the cabin. Once I opened the door, I'd start letting water into the aircraft. As long as it remained airtight, it wasn't going to sink.

Before I opened the door, I returned to the rear of the cabin. It took me a couple of minutes, but I found the emergency flares. I piled the flares, fire extinguisher, and the raft together with the Glock and knife I stole from Connors's men. Despite another look through the cockpit, I found no sign of the phone.

The plane continued to stay afloat, but I thought it might be slowly sinking. Likely, the engine compartment wasn't airtight. Water had a way of finding its way into any place. It was equally possible that the cabin wasn't airtight either.

After some time, I opened the door. The bottom of the hatch sat about six inches below the surface of the sea. The water outside wasn't high enough to create too much resistance, and I pulled the lever with my shoulder against the door. As soon as the door swung outward, seawater flooded into the aircraft. I tossed the rubber raft through the door, pulling the cord simultaneously. The CO_2 cartridge popped, and the raft whistled as air filled the chambers. Within two minutes, the entire raft inflated, unfolding itself as it did. Water filled the plane up to my knees now.

I tossed the supplies I'd gathered into the raft. Then I checked the Glock I still carried. While it was unlikely any more trouble would charge me at this point, it had been a long couple of days. Better safe and not sorry. I scrambled into the boat, and it drifted a few feet from the plane.

For what felt like the first time in days, I dropped back against the side of the craft and sighed with some relief. From the raft, I saw the lights on the shore. In the dark, I struggled to be exact, but I thought I crashed about three to four miles offshore. That was good. I should make my way to land without much problem.

Exhaustion snuck up on me, leaving me not quite ready to move just yet. The last real sleep I'd had was in the burrow on the dried creek bed. I felt a sense of relief to be back on the water with an open sky above me. I rarely realized how little I liked being on land until something forced me to do it. Plus, with the gentle breeze coming in from the Gulf, the bugs weren't bothering me. Nothing biting me at all.

It took me fifteen minutes to get moving. While my body ached, I didn't have the luxury of waiting too long. Rikki was still in trouble. If Connors kept her alive. Once Connors left the ground, it would be easy to open the aircraft door somewhere over the Gulf of Mexico and drop Rikki out.

No point thinking that way.

When on a mission, certain rules guided my actions. The target was the only thing that mattered. When a man fell, we couldn't take the time to mourn him. We kept going. Now, though, Rikki was the objective. To worry if she was still alive would be pointless. Until I received confirmation, I had to work on the assumption that Connors kept her alive.

Now it wouldn't matter to him either way. This would end with me putting a bullet between his eyes.

The lifeboat had a short paddle with it. I leaned over the edge and slowly paddled the inflatable toward the shore. With a two-foot oar, the progress was beyond slow. Shaped like a pentagon, the boat wasn't designed to move—just to float. Stroke after stroke pushed me a little farther, although when I glanced up at the shoreline, the lights felt just as far away as they had half an hour earlier.

While I rowed, my brain worked on the details of what was coming next. Sam had a private plane ready. Before I got in the air, I needed to reach out to Scar to see if he came up with any answers for me. Connors thought he was a big shot, dealing with cartels and drug lords. He imagined escaping to Mexico was far enough to get away. This world was smaller than most people expected. I'd been on every continent on the globe, and if I was pressed, I could get to any spot on Earth within a day.

No, Connors only had a head start. But what was going to screw him was his overconfidence. Of course, that worried me for Rikki too. As long as he thought I might come for him, he had an incentive to keep her alive. Once he grew complacent, he wouldn't want to deal with her.

Keep rowing.

A sharp horn blasted behind me, and I jerked up suddenly. The dark outline of a boat floated on the water. Near the plane. Someone was shining a spotlight on the water around the Cessna.

I grabbed one of the flares and fired it into the sky. The trail of red flamed in an arc upward, lighting up the raft with a red glow. The spotlight turned toward me. It wasn't strong enough to reach this far, but it lifted off the water, following the remnants of the flaming tail the flare left.

Several minutes passed before the outline of the boat started moving. It turned slowly until it was on a direct heading for me.

I waited another couple of minutes before firing the second flare into the sky, letting the captain know he was on the right path.

As the yacht drew closer, I recognized the lines. The name *Talitha* appeared on its bow as it slowed near me. Sam Cornell stepped out on the foredeck and shone the spotlight down on me.

"You survived," he called out.

"Only the good die young," I replied.

He hurried down to the lower deck, where he tossed a line off the edge toward me. I paddled the boat toward where the end hit the water and grabbed the rope. Then I dropped back into the bottom of the boat as Sam reeled me to the swim platform on the back of the yacht.

26

"Yeah," Esteban Velasquez answered.

"It's me," I told him.

"Tried to call you back a couple of hours ago," he told me. "The phone rang straight to voicemail—it wasn't your voicemail."

"No, I borrowed the phone and then I crashed a plane."

The enforcer didn't respond. "It's Las Higuerillas," he said.

"What?"

"The village you asked about. It's Las Higuerillas. It's on a little—what do you call it? Like an island."

"A key?" I questioned.

"Starts with an A."

I rolled my eyes. "Archipelago?"

"Yeah, that."

"Esteban, it's late."

I could almost hear his nonchalant shrug as he point out, "You called me."

"Right, sorry. Where is it?"

"Just south of South Padre on the Mexican coast."

"How do you know that's it?" I asked.

"It's where the heroin comes from."

"Who's shipping it in?" I asked.

"The Soria Cartel."

"What?" I asked, astonished. "They should all be dead."

"It seems you missed a few."

A couple of years earlier, I had a run-in with the Soria Cartel when they killed a woman I'd gotten involved with. Thanks to Julio Moreno and Scar, I found their family estate where I infiltrated it. After a long bloody night, I escaped, leaving the entire Soria family dead. At least, I thought I had.

"Who is running the family?"

"The daughter. Marisa. It seems she is rebuilding the little empire."

"With heroin," I remarked.

"And people," Scar added. "She's in the business of trafficking women, mostly girls."

"Ugh!" I groaned.

"It is dishonorable," Scar acknowledged. "Mr. Moreno holds no goodwill for people like that."

It was tantamount to an all-clear from his boss. Not that it mattered what he told me, but at least this way, Moreno might consider the removal of a business rival enough for this favor. He wasn't someone I enjoyed owing favors to. However, he had access to better information than I could get elsewhere.

"How many men does she have?" I asked.

"I can't say," Velazquez confessed. "Most of the men working for the Sorias vanished or moved to other cartels. Right now, she is staying under the radar. Part of why she picked a tiny fishing village to work out of."

"Thanks."

"Can I go to sleep now?" he asked me.

"Yes," I replied, but not before the line went dead.

Before returning the phone to Sam, I opened Google Maps, typing in Las Higuerillas. The image zoomed down to the little coastal town. There was only one road into the town from the north, and it crossed miles of small islands. The closest airstrip was on the mainland across the sound called *Laguna Madre*. If

Connors found a car, it would still take him three hours to get into the little fishing village.

"Chase," Sam called, interrupting my thoughts. The Irishman approached me, carrying a duffel bag.

I looked up from the phone.

"The pilot is ready to take off," he told me.

"Thanks. It's a little fishing village called Las Higuerillas," I explained to Sam, pointing to the town on the phone's screen.

"He can take you anywhere," Sam assured me. "I've already arranged it."

"Sam, the people that have her," I started. "Well, I learned something more about them just now."

"What is it, son?" he questioned.

"They are into human slavery," I said.

"Scum!" he spat. "Just find her."

While the idea of human traffickers disgusted me, it meant that Rikki might hold more value alive than dead. As long as I got there before they moved her again.

"I've put some clean clothes on board for you," Sam told me. "There's a shower and some food. You'll need to get some rest."

I nodded. "I'll find her," I promised.

He clasped my shoulder without a word. The duffel bag shifted from his hand to mine. "This could come in handy," he informed me.

I took the tote with a nod. Once I was on the plane, I'd look inside to see what he brought me.

"Can you make sure *Carina* is secure?" I asked as I started up the steps.

"Of course," he agreed.

The pilot stood in the cabin when I entered. The man was a few inches shorter than me, with almost shaggy blond hair. He lifted an eyebrow when he saw me step aboard. The sandals I stole from Connors's house slipped off me in the plane crash, and my clothes, though dry, had a distinct odor of salt water.

"Hello, I'm Captain Green," he greeted me. "Do you have the details of where we are going? Mr. Cornell told me you would know that."

"Yes," I agreed, showing him the map.

"I'll need a couple of minutes to plot a course. We should be underway soon."

"Do I have time to freshen up?" I asked.

He shook his head. "I understand you are in a hurry."

"Yes."

"We'll be airborne in ten minutes. If you can wait until we are at a cruising altitude, you can get a shower then."

"I'll take a seat then," I replied.

After settling into a soft leather chair, I stared out the window into the dark. The duffel bag Sam gave me rested on my lap. After unzipping it, I found two M45s and ten extra magazines already loaded. Two boxes of forty-five-caliber hollow-point rounds hid at the bottom of the bag. Two stacks of pesos were bound with rubber bands along with a stack of hundred-dollar bills. Sam wanted to make sure I had everything I needed.

Both forty-fives appeared in fine condition upon inspection. I replaced them in the bottom of the bag, adding the Glock I had on my waist along with the three extra nine-millimeter magazines. The duffel bag dropped to the floor, and I pushed it under my seat with my heel.

My stomach rumbled. Sam promised me food, but I'd wait a few minutes until we were airborne.

The pilot's voice came over the plane's speaker system. "We are about to take off. Please take your seat."

I'd already taken mine, so I fastened the seatbelt before letting my head lean back against the headrest. Nearly instantly, I drifted to sleep. Insomnia was never an issue for me. If I could sleep under a pile of sticks in the woods, doing so in a soft reclining chair would be no issue.

When I opened my eyes, the pilot announced I could move around. I found the lavatory where a small shower offered me the first chance to be clean in several days. After a thorough scrubbing, I dressed in the clothes Sam provided. It looked like he shopped at the nearest Army surplus store. A pair of canvas fatigues and a black t-shirt with steel-toed combat boots. He even provided two pairs of socks.

Before I dressed, I cleaned the wound on my chest and arm, re-bandaging them. Once I slipped into the fatigues, I attached the knife I'd taken off the cop to my waist. I found some lunch meat and bread, which formed into a nice sandwich that I washed down with three bottles of water. Once the rumbling stomach was sated, I plopped back into the seat. The internal clock in my head said it was 3:30 or so. As I reclined the seat back, I fell asleep.

I awoke again four hours and thirty-seven minutes later. The sun rose at our back, reflecting off the wings. I reached over and closed the window shade before pulling myself out of the seat.

In the galley, I found a coffee maker. By the time it brewed a small pot, the pilot announced we were beginning our descent. With the cup in my hand, I returned to my seat and buckled up.

The cup was empty by the time the wheels touched down on the ragged asphalt runway. I opened the shade again during the landing to study the terrain. We passed over the archipelago and the lagoon. From up here, I made out the dirt roads and small houses along the strip of land. The pale blue waters were beautiful. If I'd been on *Carina*, I could imagine dropping anchor here for a month or more. The crystal-clear, shallow waters would provide decent snorkeling and fishing. There might even be some good diving around here. It had the lazy feel I enjoy.

Seeing all the boats on the lagoon gave me an idea. Once I was off the jet, I stared across what constituted a tarmac at the El

Mezquite Airstrip. There were a couple of small cargo planes, but the only luxury plane was the one I'd just disembarked.

There was a small building on the far side of the airport. As I walked toward it, the jet began taxiing around to take off again. The deal Sam struck was that the pilot didn't remain longer than it took me to get off. Since we were skirting Mexican immigration and customs, it seemed advisable to get the plane back into US airspace before anyone noticed it. El Mezquite's only air traffic control comprised a small radio antenna and a singule radio operator.

The man in question stood in the doorway of the small shack, watching me approach.

"*Carro?*" I asked, motioning with my hands as if I was turning a steering wheel—the universal sign for car.

The man glanced over at the 1986 Mazda B2000 pickup parked next to the building. He shook his head, and I pulled a hundred-dollar bill out.

"I need a ride to Mezquite," I said, again using the sign for car.

All of my Spanish skills were developed in the tenth grade of high school. Now I could ask where the bathroom was and order a beer, but that was the extent to which I could communicate. Given that I lived in South Florida and enjoyed traveling to some islands where Spanish was the official language, I should attempt to learn more of it. It would come in more handy than the Pashto I learned in Afghanistan.

The short, disheveled man stared at the bill. It was likely worth more than two weeks of work for him. The trip to the village of Mezquite was only a couple of miles.

"*Solo a Mezquite.*"

"Near *la laguna*?" I asked, and the man reached out and took the bill before marching to the blue truck. When I got to the cab, I paused. The passenger seat held cases of bottled water. I wondered if his little office lacked running water. He made a gesture that he'd move the water, but I waved him off, tossing my duffel in the truck's bed. My hands caught the edge, and I jumped up into the back end, giving the man a grin and a thumbs-up.

He climbed into the driver's seat and drove along a dirt road that no one had graded in a decade. The Mazda bounced back and forth, jarring me around the back. I gripped the edge, trying to stay on the wheel well. When he reached the main highway, it was only moderately better than the gravel one. Over the years, the thin layer of asphalt had been worn down, leaving potholes as wide as the truck.

To call Mezquite a village would have been a promotion in its status. The community comprised six buildings, three of which appeared occupied. Four young boys played soccer with a sun-bleached ball. The match paused long enough for the kids to wave at the passing truck. I thought I heard one child shout "Papa," leading me to think my chauffeur might live there. The driver waved at the boys before blasting his horn with two quick beeps.

We drove another five minutes before the road seemed to end at the water's edge. Several flat-bottomed fishing boats rested on the bank.

"*¿Aquí?*" the man asked as he climbed out of the cab.

"*Sí,*" I replied. "Whose boats are these?" My hand gestured at the ones on the rocky waterfront.

He pointed down the shore at a man a few hundred yards away wading knee-deep into the lagoon. The older man vigorously hurled a net out into the water, letting it spread into a wide circle before it hit the surface. Weights along the edge dragged the net to the bottom, trapping any fish that might be in its grasp. The old guy reeled the rope in, dragging the netting back with whatever bounty came with it. He dumped the fish into a white bucket and threw it again.

I gave the driver a nod. "*Gracias,*" I told him.

"*De nada*," he said, absentmindedly touching his shirt pocket where the hundred-dollar bill disappeared earlier.

He pulled a bottle of water out and tossed it to me.

"*Gracias.*"

He smiled and climbed into the cab of the Mazda B2000 and backed up until he could turn around. I watched the cloud of dust trail behind the truck as he headed back to his shack.

I slipped the bottle of water into the side pocket of my fatigues before I walked along the shore to the fisherman. He glanced up at me as I approached.

"*Hola*," I called, waving.

"*Hola*," he responded warily, probably wondering what a *gringo* wanted from him.

I pulled another hundred-dollar bill from my pocket. My hand extended the money to him. Cautiously, he took the cash from me, staring at it for a second before glancing up at me.

"That's yours," I explained slowly in English.

The old man's scratchy voice responded, "What do you want?"

I gave him a smile and pulled out another bill. "I need to get across the lagoon."

27

Laguna Madre separated the barrier islands from the mainland of Mexico. The aluminum boat buzzed slowly across the choppy water. The old man who told me his name was Felix, sat in the back of the craft, steering with a tiller handle on the nine-horsepower motor. Most of what I'd seen in the lagoon indicated the depth here was very shallow—only two to three feet deep. Definitely too skinny for *Carina* to anchor in here. The little dots I saw from the plane now revealed themselves as similar-style fishing boats. We passed a few fishermen who offered Felix a courteous wave and a smile. It was always nice to see that the culture of boat people was the same around the world. As Randy, the dockmaster at the Tilly Marina where I park *Carina,* explained to me that he referred to boaters who don't wave to others as a "Boatholes." Generally, I found his assessment accurate.

Felix spoke English well, telling me he'd worked up in Corpus Christi for fifteen years on a shrimping boat. His son married a local Texan girl, and they moved to Dallas. He didn't see them often, but they sent cards regularly.

Now that we were running the throttle wide open, our conversation ceased, and we both watched the water while staying consumed in our own thoughts.

My own mind wondered what I was going to find on the other side of the lake. Marisa Soria was rebuilding her family's empire after I burned it down. Did she know who did that to her? After I was stateside, I heard the rumors that a rival cartel crushed the Soria Cartel. However, when I left their estate, there were few, if any, survivors who might have seen me during that evening.

If Marisa Soria knew I was the responsible party, I suspect she'd have attempted to render her idea of justice on me already.

My right hand reached over the gunwale, dipping into the water. A small wake formed behind my fingers as they skimmed through the surface. When I pulled them out, I touched my tongue. The salinity tasted stronger than normal, but the salt offered a weird comfort for me. It wasn't drinkable, but something about the salty water of the ocean strengthened me.

Over my shoulder, I studied the old fisherman. Felix was only in his sixties, but a life on the water left him dark and pitted from the weather. Yet, he smiled as his face lifted into the breeze while he breathed in the freedom of the sea.

The trip took about 107 minutes. When Felix cut the outboard off, the sudden silence engulfed us for six seconds before the aluminum hull scraped across the rocky shore.

"You don't look like a fisherman," Felix commented as I grabbed my duffel bag. "There's only two things going on in this village."

"Really?" I asked. "What can you tell me about it?"

Felix lifted an eyebrow. "You seem *simpático*—nice, but also like someone ready to fight."

I shrugged.

"Are you a good person?" Felix asked.

"That could be debatable," I answered. "But I try to be."

"There are people in Las Higuerillas who are not good people."

"Cartel?" I asked.

The old fisherman nodded. "They came in last year. I stay on that side of *La Madre*," he explained. "*Es peligroso*. Very dangerous."

"Some might say the same thing about me," I told him.

Felix appraised me before saying, "*Sí*, I believe so."

"Thank you for the ride," I told him as I climbed out onto the rocky beach.

"Will you need to go back?" he asked.

I turned and looked north along the chalky white shoreline. My head shook. "No, I'll be finding a different way out of here."

He dipped his chin slightly. "*Buena suerte.*"

I only understood that *buena* meant "good." Maybe he said "Good luck." Or possibly "Good riddance." All I did was nod to him as I turned to march up the slope.

Felix dropped me on the north shore of the pass leading out to the Gulf. He'd chosen an isolated beach. Based on his warning, I suspected he didn't want to be spotted by the local criminal element. He struck me as a perceptive guy, and if someone saw him drop off the only gringo around, they might remember that if trouble started.

The hike to the road took about fifteen minutes, most of that spent navigating the rocky incline. By the time I reached the streets, I was dripping with sweat. The back of my hand wiped the beads of perspiration from my face before I slung the droplets to the ground.

Once I found the gravel road, I walked another half an hour up the virtually empty lane. I passed the port control where a small freighter docked. A couple of men loaded the boat with crates. Neither man gave me a look as I trudged past. This was an area where no one appreciated questions, so people didn't bother to ask them, even to themselves.

I stopped at a two-story white and red building. A balcony wrapped around the second level over arched openings. An aroma of freshly cooked something drifted out the opened windows. A hand-painted sign read "Cafetel." There were several old trucks from the early nineties parked in the dirt lot. I adjusted the shoulder strap from my duffel bag and started for the door.

When I stepped through a propped door, the sound of sizzling and the more acute fragrance of shrimp cooking smacked my senses. Although neither of those overpowered the stares directed at me from the eight men seated around the small room. A crude bar built from plywood and particle board and painted a bright turquoise stretched along the far side of the room. Open windows offered a breezy view of the blue lagoon behind it. A short, dark-haired woman in her forties scurried down the bar, carrying a bottle of beer.

When I settled on the corner stool, the woman walked down to me with a confused look on her face. She wore a faded shirt with the mouth and tongue logo of the Rolling Stones.

"*¿Quieres beber algo?*"

"*Cerveza.*" Like I said, I knew enough Spanish to order a beer.

"Indio," I added, pointing at the sign on a clock over the bar that read the wrong time.

"*Sí,*" the woman replied. She reached into a plastic fifty-five-gallon drum filled with bottles of beer and ice.

When she handed me the bottle, I touched the glass that dripped with ice-cold water which pooled on the turquoise bar.

"*¿Habla inglés?*" I asked in what little I recalled from my tenth-grade Spanish class.

"Not good," she offered.

"Menu?" I asked.

She handed me a worn page with faded pictures. One picture I could make out said "*Camarones de Diablo.*" My index finger touched that line. "Can I have that one?"

"*Sí.*"

I drank the rest of the Indio beer, and when the woman eyed me, I gave her the universal sign for "another beer." She returned with another cold bottle, and I took a little longer sipping this one. Staring out the window, it occurred to me that an icy beer on a beach might be the best definition of heaven. If I didn't have an agenda, this spot right here would occupy me for several hours.

"What is your name?" I asked the bartender.

She gave a cursory scan of the room at the other faces sitting around the café. "Angela," she answered, giving the G the Spanish H sound.

Angela migrated to the other end of the bar where two brawny, tall men sat nursing a couple of cans of Modelo over two empty plates. Both men focused on me. They murmured in Spanish to Angela, who made a gesture I interpreted as "don't start shit." It wasn't one of those universal signs like "driving" or "another one." This was more in the language I understood—bartender. Trouble in her bar meant more work for her. Those two struck me as regulars, but then, in a town the size of a thumbnail, everyone would be a regular.

She returned a few minutes later carrying a plate of food. A hefty pile of shrimp tossed in a red sauce filled most of the dish with a mound of rice and black beans.

"*Gracia*," I said.

She nodded. "*¿Más cerveza, señor?*"

"*Sí.*"

This needed to be my last one if I was going to keep my head about myself. Luckily, I'd sweat out most of it in minutes. Angela returned with another Indio, and I ate in silence, fully aware the two men at the end of the bar hadn't taken their eyes off me.

The sauce on the shrimp carried plenty of spice, and I took a few big swallows of beer to wash down the heat. When I finished eating, I rested my fork on the bar and pushed the plate away. Angela came back again, reaching for the plate.

"Angela, I need some help."

She cocked her head. Her expression—curious. What did the gringo want?

"Where can I find Marisa Soria?"

I watched her catch her breath. Her eyes cut to the two guys at the end of the bar. "*No sé.*"

"*Gracias*. How much?"

"*Doscientos pesos.*"

Guessing that "*dos*" probably meant two hundred, I gave her three hundred peso notes. She forced a smile. Any congenial manner she had vanished at the mention of Marisa Soria. I got to my feet, slipped the duffel over my shoulder, and started down to the opposite end.

"*¿Señores, habla inglés?*" I almost cringed, wondering if I was even close to saying the correct thing.

The one on the left reminded me of a Latino actor whose name I couldn't place. He gave a curt nod. "What do you want?"

I offered a slight smile. "Can I buy you a beer?"

He cut his eyes to the other man, a taller man with a homemade tattoo etched into his skin. The image might have been a crow or raven. Whoever inked it on him didn't do him any favors. The distorted bird was supposed to be taking flight, but it could have been sprawled on the asphalt like roadkill.

Crow replied, "Yeah, we'll drink a beer."

"Angela, *dos cervezas* down here."

She pulled two cans of Modelo out of the beer drum and walked them down to the men.

"Let me ask you a question, guys," I said. "I'm looking for the house of Marisa Soria."

Both men stared at me. "We don't know this person."

"Guys, c'mon. I've heard she lives here. It seems unlikely no one knows where she is."

The actor-looking one shook his head slowly. "We don't know this name."

I pulled out another hundred-dollar bill, holding it between two fingers.

"Why don't we just take all of those?" Crow questioned, pushing up off his stool.

"That wouldn't be advisable," I explained as the other man stood.

Angela shouted something in Spanish. Crow retorted, and while I didn't understand it, I bet it was along the lines of "shut up."

"Hand it all over, and we won't hurt you," the first one demanded, reaching for the bill still in my hand.

I took a step back, forcing them to step around the corner to reach me. My initial assessment suggested that Crow was the alpha male of the two. The actor was a follower, and he'd do whatever Crow suggested.

Then Crow made the suggestion in Spanish. The actor made his move, lunging his right arm toward me. My left hand flew up, catching his wrist and twisting it around. I slammed the back of his hand against the top of the bar. While my left hand pinned his arm, my right came up with the knife from my belt. The blade drove down into the man's palm, nailing it to the plywood.

I released the handle and threw my elbow into Crow's face. The blow wasn't effective, but the brutality of my attack on his friend shocked Crow. He didn't prepare for the elbow, and his head popped back. My body twisted on my right heel, and I drove my left fist into Crow's face. The cartilage in his nose gave way under my knuckles, and the man dropped back onto his ass.

The actor howled in pain, and I turned back, wrenching the blade out of his hand. He immediately withdrew his arm, cradling his wounded hand. I saw what was about to happen, stepping back as he vomited his lunch and Modelo on Crow, who was trying to get back to his feet.

Crow let out a string of Spanish words. Even without a translator, I recognized the tone of cursing in any language.

Angela rattled away too, pointing at the door and shouting at me. I took the hundred-dollar bill and folded it up, replacing it in my pocket.

28

Kicked out of the café, I stood back on the streets of Las Higuerillas. The Mexican sun reflected off the white gravel and whiter buildings. I suppose the thought process followed that the reflective color of the town would cut down on the heat in each building. What did I know, though?

From the outside, the village made the perfect hideaway for the Soria gang. It was difficult to get to and offered almost no amenities. The townsfolk subsisted on fishing. That much was obvious. Old boats with patch jobs lined the streets. Most didn't have motors, having found forced retirement after the leaks became unmanageable. This wasn't even a beach getaway for some of the larger cities. The houses were small, some nothing more than cinderblock shacks with tin roofs.

A skinny brown dog full of milk moseyed up beside me. She sniffed my legs for a bit before I relented, kneeling down to scratch her behind the ears. When she realized I wasn't offering any food, she ambled away with a somewhat frustrated air about her.

The streets were surprisingly empty. Although it was midday—siesta. I trudged along a half mile before I saw anyone on the street. A twenty-something young male stripped down a motor of an older Toyota Tacoma. The once-red truck sat on makeshift jack stands fashioned out of broken concrete blocks.

The man rolled out from under the vehicle with a fuel pump in his hand.

"*Hola,*" I greeted him. "*¿Dondé esta las Sorias?*"

The butchering of the language I'd just performed embarrassed me. The kid stared at me for a second, and I wondered if my Spanish was that bad. He only shook his head as if he had no response. His face told a different story, though. He knew what I asked, but he wasn't about to be the guy to give me the answer.

"You don't know Marisa Soria?" I figured if the locals couldn't understand ninety-five percent of what I was saying, the name of the head of the local cartel would be the part they did.

His eyes widened before he turned away, waving me off as he moved to his toolbox.

I moved away, leaving the kid to his work. He didn't offer me much information—except that the town feared the Sorias.

Ahead on the left, I spotted a small building with a neon Modelo sign. Another bar seemed like a good place to continue my prodding. I figured in a village this size word would reach *Casa de Soria* that a gringo was wandering about the community asking for Marisa Soria. Crow and his wounded *amigo* likely already sent up the first flare.

The inside of the next little saloon was fractional compared to Angela's Cafetel. A single gray-haired man in his sixties leaned on the back of the bar watching a thirty-two inch television broadcasting a soccer match. He glanced up as I came in, surprised at the business during the day.

I pointed at a Sol Cerveza mirror hanging above the bottles of liquor and asked, "*¿Cerveza?*"

Again, my grasp of Spanish delivered a cold Sol bottle to the bar. "Do you speak English?" I asked the bartender, setting my duffel bag on top of the empty bar.

"No," he stated.

"*¿Dondé esta las Sorias?*" I repeated the question I'd mangled with the young mechanic earlier.

The bartender's brows raised. "*Usted no quiere las Sorias.*" The tone of his voice sounded either threatening or dire. Perhaps a bit of both.

"*Necesito habla con Marisa Soria,*" I said, continuing to butcher the language.

The man shook his head. "*Cuidado. La Señorita Soria es muy peligrosa.*"

This time I was sure he was cautioning me. I lifted the beer in a singular toast to the man. A signal, I hoped, that I wasn't worried about whatever warning he offered. If there was one thing I'd learned, it was that the more brazen a person was, the more likely they'd draw the opposition's attention. It worked better if there was a mutual language, but I worked with what I'd got.

The man nodded once to me as he returned to his soccer game. I nursed the beer, studying the bar. There were three tables spread around the tight area, which, if including the bar, allowed a max of sixteen customers. An old purple radio from the mid-nineties sat on a shelf above the bar. It was one of those that had speakers that detached from the main body and stretched a few feet away if the speaker cable was long enough. It reminded me of one my sister, Jocelyn, had in junior high. She'd take it out and separate the speakers as far as she could. Her reasoning was that it allowed the sound to surround her. I smiled at the thought of her dancing to Britney Spears like she was trying to pay her bills.

A shadow filled the entry, and I sensed a presence behind me. Without turning around, I glanced at the reflection in the Sol mirror. Three men stepped through the open door. Right off the bat, I noticed these guys were cut from a different mold than Crow and his friend. They almost smelled like trouble. Plus, they were the cleanest trio of people I'd seen in this town.

"Who are you?" a voice asked behind me. The baritone question came from the man in the middle of the group.

I sipped the Sol, watching them from the corner of my eye in the sign's reflection.

"I'm here on business," I replied. "With Marisa Soria."

"What kind of business?" the man asked.

My eyes shifted to the bartender, who cowered at the farthest edge. He locked gazes with me, saying the unspoken, "I told you so." Or whatever that would translate to Spanish. I responded by cutting my eyes to a rear exit, hoping he understood my warning to get out of here. He inched along the wall to the door, heeding my silent advice.

The M45s were still in my duffel bag—a possible mistake on my part. I twisted around on the barstool. It would have been more dramatic if the seat swiveled. Instead, the legs screeched as I shifted the seat around to face the trio.

"Are you Marisa Soria?" I asked, taking another drink from my bottle of beer.

"No," the middle man said. He stared at me with black, beady eyes.

All three of the men looked like they'd gone shopping in the same catalog Scar did. They each wore snakeskin boots that cost more than this building did. Beady Eyes wore a black shirt with silver buttons. Both of the others wore different shades of blue. The man on the right, though, had a round gambler-style hat. On the left, the tough guy sported a thin moustache and slicked-back oily hair.

"Well, I guess my business isn't with you."

"We work for Señorita Soria," the Gambler stated.

"Great," I replied, sliding off the stool. My steel-toed boots clunked on the wood slat floor. "Why don't you take me to her?"

Beady Eyes shook his head. "Not until you tell us what you want."

My right hand gripped the Sol bottle tighter just before I lunged it upward. The mouth of the bottle slammed into Beady Eye's esophagus, causing him to emit an aching gasp as his throat crushed. My wrist twisted as I stepped back. With a snap of my arm, I drove the bottom of the half-drank beer into Slick's eye. The Gambler hadn't had time to register what happened, and he reacted a split second too late as the toe of my boot caught him in the groin with enough force to lift him off his feet.

The knife came off my belt, and the razor edge dug into Slick's throat just enough to draw blood. Still stunned from the glass bottle to the face, his brain moved slow. When he saw the trickle of blood from his throat in the mirrored Sol sign, he stopped moving.

Beady Eyes thrashed on the floor, desperate for oxygen that couldn't pass through his damaged throat. Gambler straightened up, having recovered from the kick. He pulled a Hipoint nine-millimeter.

There wasn't enough time to decide if the Gambler and Slick were close enough to bargain for each other's life. The knife slashed across Slick's throat as I lunged at the black barrel moving in my direction. My entire body moved past the Gambler's reach, driving him into the cinderblock wall. His hat fell off his head as we collided with the side of the room. The gunshot echoed through the building as a bottle behind the bar exploded.

Gambler shoved against me, pushing me off him for a second. My forehead slammed into his face, knocking the back of his skull against the concrete wall with a thud. The blow to the head stunned him, and I caught the nine-millimeter with my left hand, jerking it out of his grip. I took a step back, raising the crappy gun to the man's face. He stared up the barrel at my narrowed glare.

Behind me, a bubbling gurgle sounded as the air in Slick's lungs escaped through the gash. He realized he was out of cards.

"Did Marisa send you?" I inquired.

His eyes cut around the room as if one of his dead buddies might rise from the dirty floor to aid him. Finally, he nodded.

"Where is she?" I asked calmly.

"North on this road. There's a drive on the ocean side."

The first gunshot startled Gambler more than me. The hairs on my neck straightened, or maybe I glimpsed them moving outside the open door. Whatever it was, I twisted around, diving over the bar. As the inside of the cantina rang with gunfire, I reached over the top of the counter, dragging my duffel down with me. In eight seconds, I had both M45s in my hands. Glass and liquid rained down on my head as bullets riddled the saloon.

After half a minute, the barrage of gunfire ceased. From the floor behind the bar, I could only see the splintered remains of tequila and whiskey bottles. The Sol mirror still hung to the wall, but the glass shattered in pieces. Only two jagged sections remained in the frame. Those tiny bits offered me a view of the top of the door.

I waited in silence. A groan off to the side interrupted the calm. Gambler must have caught a few rounds. Friendly fire, I suppose.

The floor creaked as the first foot stepped into the building. The shadows on the wall darkened as the gunmen blocked the sunlight in the door. Checking the mirror, I popped up, rotating around. Both M45s fired in my hand in rapid succession. The gunmen in the front of the room fell as my rounds tore through their faces. Each of them still held their weapons up, but the killing shots eliminated any chance of them returning fire.

I dropped back down, in case there were more outside. Again, it was quiet, except for the sound of dying thugs. After thirty seconds ticked by, I used the mirror to check the room. It was clear.

As I stood up, I turned to survey the saloon. The three gunmen laid in the doorway. One of them twitched in his last death throes. Gambler leaned against the wall. His chest bloodied and chewed up. I swapped the magazines out for the full ones and slipped the spares into the cargo pocket of my fatigues. Both M45s fit into the side pockets like holsters, and I tucked the Glock under my waistband. I left the duffel bag with several thousand dollars still in the satchel for the poor bar owner.

From here on, I didn't think I'd need any money.

The palms of both hands rested on the grips of the forty-fives as I walked out of the bar into the street.

29

If I thought the street was quiet before the shootout, now it seemed like a vacuum. Even the breeze I'd felt hiking in from the waterfront was gone. A few squeaks and creaks sounded from the buildings. A tumbleweed rolling past me would seem apropos.

I followed Gambler's directions. Every house I strolled past looked like someone had sealed it permanently shut. Hurricane shutters were closed. The exterior wooden doors that protected the smaller framed entryways leading into the homes were locked up. If I didn't know any better, I'd be expecting a storm front to wallop the coast.

Instead, it seemed like the locals who tolerated the lady Soria's new business endeavor had no intention of sticking their necks out too far.

The end of the gravel road led me to a pebbled concrete drive, where a twelve-foot cinder-block wall stood, constructed along the road front. A twenty-four-foot-wide gate made of wrought iron blocked the entrance. The spires of each metal spike corkscrewed toward the sky.

To beautify the gray blocks making up the barrier around the property, someone painted a coral reef mural with several brightly colored fish. A tiger shark swam harmlessly through the sea life, its body frozen in a sharp twist.

If the twelve-foot climb over the wall wasn't enough of a deterrent, six strands of razor wire stretched across the top. Anyone scaling to the top would find themselves sliced to pieces as they proceeded over. It didn't allow for an ideal incursion, to say the least.

Besides, while I didn't locate any, I expected there were closed-circuit cameras watching the perimeter. I stood in front of the gate. On the opposite side of the metal fencing, I could see *casa de Soria*. A recently renovated two-story house stood overlooking the shore. Covered by the typical stucco found in this area, the outside gleamed white under the recent paint. A wraparound promenade offered a 360-degree view from the second floor. Arched openings along the walkways gave the homeowners a breezy veranda where they could do pretty much anything alfresco.

The metal gates groaned as the control arm swung outward. I stepped away, pulling the forty-fives from my pants as two men charged around the corner at me. Each had an automatic rifle they were raising. I shot one and dove away as the other opened fire. Bullets raced after me, and I returned fire. Before the man took another shot, a figure appeared from the side, tackling me. My forty-five skittered across the ground from my left hand.

My grip on the other gun stayed tight as my assailant grappled with me on the concrete. As we rolled to the left, I squeezed off one round. The shot was only about twenty-five percent luck as the bullet struck the man with the rifle in the shin. From the corner of my eye, I watched him topple over as the bone shattered in his lower leg.

Unfortunately, the guy on top of me had me in a position where I couldn't get free. He wrapped his legs around my midriff in some sort of judo move. He fought my right hand as I attempted to swing the M45 into his head. I bucked my waist up, trying to throw him to the side, but he countered with his weight.

As I tried to pull my right arm loose, he redoubled his efforts to hold it down, using both arms. My left hand struck him with a spearhand just under the ribs. The blow knocked the air out of his lungs for a second, and I jerked around, pulling the knife off my belt. The blade stabbed into his side.

He growled in agony as the point of the knife tore through some vital organs. I rotated the handle, tearing through his intestines. With another buck, I dislodged the wounded man, rolling him over with my hand still on the knife.

As he flopped onto his side, I saw the man I'd shot in the leg raising up with his rifle. My hand found the Glock at the small of my back, whipping it around. I shot him as he fired a burst. A round grazed the top of my shoulder, ripping through the skin. I twisted around, rolling to the ground. It took me a second to realize the wound was only superficial as I rotated my arm freely.

Pushing off the drive, I saw two more men appear at the gate. They trained their rifles on me. I threw the Glock away, raising my hand.

"I would like to speak with Marisa Soria!" I shouted.

The man in the front called to the house in Spanish. Then he stared down the barrel of his LSAT LMG at me. "Who are you?" the man asked.

"That's for Señorita Soria," I answered.

"Then you do not see *La Señorita*," the gunman explained.

I cocked my head to the side as three more gunmen appeared, carrying more LSATs. The light machine guns they carried looked like military issue, which was likely since they were initially manufactured for the US military. That didn't make it impossible for the rest of the world to get them. Hell, we left enough equipment in Afghanistan to supply several cartels.

The three men moved around me, splitting away from a tight formation to cover me from three angles. They kept a moderate distance of about twelve feet between me and them. Even if I could cover the distance to one of them, the other two could gun me down before I could do anything.

My hands remained at my shoulder height as I stood up. "I would like to discuss the future of Gray Connors with her," I explained.

The lead man among the three gunmen announced, "Move forward with your hands on the back of your head."

He then said something in Spanish to the other two men—instructions, I assumed.

The fingers of both of my hands laced together on the back of my scalp. The man in charge took position on my right flank. Both of the other men marched at a distance, with the one in the lead, marching slowly backward. His LSAT directed at me the entire time.

Once we passed through the gate, it was as if they transported me to a different world. The grounds inside the cinder-block fence grew lush and green. A stone path led me along the side of the building. Colorful flowers bordered the walkway and the house, each palette chosen to meld with the other. Marble fountains and statues erected in the yard had a Renaissance revival motif.

On the back side of the house, a small pool was under construction. At the moment, the crystal-clear water invited me toward it. The mounds of sand and dirt around it indicated there was still work to be done on the walkway and deck surrounding the pool.

When the work on it finished, the pool would overlook the Gulf of Mexico. The pale blue sea sank off the shore only a couple of miles out. There the turquoise shade deepened to dark blue.

There was more recent construction added to the property. A stairwell sloped gradually to the water. Anchored just offshore, a fifty-three-foot Hatteras floated. Judging from where the steps ended, I guessed the yacht belonged to the Señorita.

The trio of guards continued to escort me to the back of the house. It impressed me that the one in the lead walked backward from the street without stumbling once. His wrinkled brow and tight stare gave away the gravity of his duty.

He opened an ornate steel door. The decorative nature of it almost masked the security aspect. Manufactured from one-inch square steel tubing, the bars were welded in a grid pattern with a curvaceous design reminding me of a fleur-de-lis. I bet the sculpture itself had been hand forged.

When we stepped inside, the cool air slapped me as if I hadn't expected air-conditioning. A long leather couch faced me with a young Latina stretched out on it. She wore a very thin red bikini. Her left thigh faced the ceiling, allowing me to see the colorful tattoo of a bird grasping a snake. She, or whoever inked her, ripped the imagery from Mexican lore. The snake could represent several gods or goddesses in the Mayan and Mexican culture. Quetzalcoatl was the one I was most familiar with, although I didn't remember the details behind his legend. I wondered if Marisa Soria knew the story. Probably. It might be like the tales of Davy Crockett or Paul Bunyan were to kids in America. No, likely they were more important symbols of their culture.

"Señorita Soria?" I asked, staring at the girl who couldn't have been over twenty-four.

"You are the man who has come into my town and started killing my employees?" she questioned, reaching toward a hand-carved table where a platter of cheese sat. She plucked a small cube of white cheese and dropped it into her mouth.

"I only asked to find you," I told her. "Your men escalated matters. All they needed to do was point me to your house."

"I tasked those men with protecting my privacy." She talked as she chewed the cheese.

My neck turned, cocking my head a bit as I watched her. "Perhaps they need a better directive," I suggested. "They could have made it a lot easier."

"Now you are here," she mused, with a bored tone. "What do you have to say to me?"

"You are working with Gray Connors."

"Is that a question?" she asked. "Or a statement?"

I offered a half-shrug.

Señorita Soria motioned for the man who led the trio into the house. "Go get me Connors."

When he marched out of the room, she stared at me. "We might as well bring in the man if we're going to talk about him."

"Of course," I replied. "My grandmother always told me to never say something about a man that you wouldn't say to his face."

"Your *abuela* sounds smart," she said with a smirk.

"I don't know. Whenever I followed that advice, it got me into a lot of fights."

Gray Connors appeared in the hallway behind the Señorita.

"Good, Gray, you're here," she simpered. "Would you like to tell me how this man followed you here?"

Connors glared at me. His eyes tightened, wrinkling the skin along his temple. "Why won't you die?" he snapped.

"I'm hoping you still have my friend, Señorita Soria."

"What friend is that?" she asked.

"The woman Connors brought with him," I explained. "If he did something with her, then I'll have no choice but to kill him."

"I'm sorry, señor, but I don't know your name. You are now quite familiar with mine. It only seems fair that I can call you something."

"For now, why don't you just call me 'Lieutenant'?"

"You are military?" she asked, lifting an eyebrow.

"Something like that," I exaggerated.

"Well, Lieutenant, I can't very well let you kill my guest and business associate under my roof. What kind of hostess would that make me?"

"First, I'd reconsider your business arrangement with Connors. The infrastructure he built in Florida is all but destroyed. By now, I suspect the DEA is sifting through his house and property. I doubt it will take them long to figure out who is sourcing the goods he was storing."

"That won't happen," Connors insisted.

I grinned. "I figured it out in less than half an hour. Imagine if I'd had the resources of the United States government."

The girl on the couch swung her legs off the cushion until her feet rested on the floor. She pushed up from her seat, rising to just about five and a half feet tall. Her dark brown eyes stared into mine as she stepped closer.

"*If* you had the resources?" she questioned.

My face winced.

"You aren't military or with the government. Are you?"

"Not currently," I remarked. "Although that didn't stop me from tearing Connors down."

The Señorita turned her head slowly to stare at the older man. "You brought him here?"

"He couldn't have followed me," Connors mumbled. "Even if he did, he's one man. We kill him and start over."

"Start over?" she asked.

"I still have all the contacts. We have a hiccup, but we can be back to running things normally within two months. Until then, I have some contingencies." Connors spoke with confidence. "I think the girl will compensate for some of your losses today."

"Where is she?" I asked.

The cartel queen stared at me. "She's fine right now."

I returned her glare. Since we came into the house, I'd only seen the three guards covering me. If Marisa Soria was still rebuilding, she might not have a lot more power to put behind her.

My eyes scanned the room. I folded my arms as I made a pretense of studying the decor.

"Are you shopping for something?" she asked me.

"I'm just wondering how much of this stuff came from the house down in Alvarado."

Marisa Soria's eyes widened, and her muscles clenched. "What are you talking about?" she demanded.

"I like the view and all here, but I really think the other house was nicer. A better piece of property."

The girl stepped closer to me, and all three guards tightened the grip on their guns, making certain I was the only one in their sights.

"How would you know anything about my father's house?"

"Obviously, I've been there," I pointed out. "But it was last year."

Her balled up fist cracked the side of my jaw. I let my head twist when she hit me.

"I'll kill you and that fucking bitch!"

30

"Just kill him," Connors pleaded. "The girl is worth something."

"Quiet!" she ordered. "If you say another word, I'll throw you on the sofa with him."

For the moment, I leaned back on the sofa, watching the spectacle in front of me. She'd ordered one of her men to bring Rikki.

The two watchdogs remained alert, with their LSATs pointed at me. Marisa Soria threw out whatever odd notion she had to allure me with the skimpy swimsuit. After demanding the guards to keep me on the couch, she slipped into a sheer robe. I wish I could have said I'd never seen a woman dress angrily, but I'll admit that this time, she had a bit more fire in her movements.

"He killed my family," she told Connors.

"That's not possible," the man explained. "What makes you think that?"

"He knows about my father's house," Marisa tried to explain. Even as she voiced it, the words made no sense to her. But she still knew I did it. Which was fine with me—the pretense grew old.

"Anyone can figure that out," Connors said. "Use your brain."

Señorita Soria's eyes burned when she stared him down. "What did I tell you about speaking?"

Connors's brain seemed finally to catch up to him, and he clamped his mouth shut.

Marisa leaned over me. "You did it, didn't you?" she questioned.

I gave her an appraising stare without uttering a sound.

The girl straightened up and marched across the room to a cabinet. "Some of these things came from my father's home. I salvaged them after the fire."

"You weren't there that night?" I asked.

Marisa removed a cutlass from the case. The steel rested on her left palm as she wrapped the fingers of her right hand around the hilt. Deftly, she wielded the sword, slicing it through the air with enough speed to allow the blade to whistle.

"No, I was in California at the time, attending Stanford."

"Stanford, huh? That's impressive."

She offered me a bitter half-smile. "The call came early the next morning from my sister-in-law. Can you imagine that? Waking up to hear that someone came and murdered your entire family? It was devastating."

I gave her a grin. "C'mon. Your family was nothing but murderers. If people got in your way, you killed them. As a college girl, haven't you heard the old saying: Live by the sword, die by the sword?"

Marisa whipped the cutlass through the air as she charged me. The edge of the blade stopped just inches from my throat. She had no intention of killing me here, though. I knew that much for certain.

If that was going to happen, she wouldn't have made a production of bringing out a sword. She'd have gunned me down right here. But she was *La Señorita*, a moniker she wanted to perpetuate. After all, Marisa was the heir to the Soria Cartel.

One didn't remain the head of a criminal organization like that without proving oneself.

Plus, there was the pomp and circumstance of the entire affair. It oozed off her. That was why she greeted me half-dressed. Marisa Soria wanted to show herself, not only to the people surrounding her but also to herself.

I gave her that opportunity. Today would be a reckoning. At this point, even if she discovered I hadn't killed her family, the moment arrived on a golden wing.

My eyes cut over to Connors. He still didn't realize today was his last day alive. After she killed Rikki before me—a way to punish me for her family, she'd behead me in the most glorious fashion. But once it was over, Marisa would take a hard look at Connors. He'd not only failed her, but he'd also brought me into her midst. Of course, that could be a bonus for the man, if he'd have done it with some forethought. Instead, Connors was nothing more than a man who'd lost everything he built because of one man. People like that didn't last too long in organizations like the cartel.

The guard who'd left to retrieve Rikki had been gone awhile—almost half an hour. She must not be in the house, but if she were too far, I'd figure Marisa would restrain me instead of continuing with her show.

Finally, the rear door opened, and Rikki stepped through with the guard and two men I assumed came with Connors based on the backwoods aura they exuded.

"Chase!" Rikki exclaimed. "What the hell are you doing here?"

"It's your rescue," I announced. "Ta-da!"

"Chase?" Marisa questioned. "We have a name. Not just Lieutenant."

"I didn't think we were on much of a get-to-know-you date here."

The girl shook her head, amused. As the minutes ticked by, she'd grown used to the idea of killing me. I doubted there was an ounce of real rage in her about her family. Perhaps it upset her when her way of life became disrupted. Who knows? She could have been a daddy's girl.

"Bring them," she ordered, letting the flat edge of the cutlass rest across her shoulder.

The chief guard motioned for me to stand up. The group marched us out the front door.

"Where is she taking us?" Rikki asked under her breath.

"I'd guess as close to the town center as this place has," I told her. "She's going to cement her standing in the community."

"By killing us?"

"Pretty much," I replied.

"They were talking about selling me to some sheik in Dubai or something."

"I think I derailed that," I said.

"Oh, good," Rikki remarked. "I hate the desert."

We reached the primary thoroughfare through town. Marisa gave one man an order in Spanish, and he ran off down the road. He shouted at the houses, continuing into the village.

"I don't understand what you're doing," Connors commented.

Before she could snap at him, doors opened. Townsfolk trickled out of their homes and into the street. Their eyes trained on our crowd with unanswered questions in their stares.

A few minutes passed and more people came back down the road. Marisa Soria lifted the cutlass in the air and let out a bloodcurdling scream. All eyes turned to her as everyone gathered fell silent.

She shouted in Spanish. Her sword jabbed toward us as she spoke, but the only word I fully understood was gringo.

"Did you understand that?" Rikki asked.

I shrugged.

"She said that we trespassed in their home, killed their fathers and brothers, and defiled the land."

"Eh, I suppose," I remarked.

"Speak for yourself," Rikki admonished. "She also said she plans to ship us back to the States in tiny boxes."

"Bring me the woman!" Marisa called, pointing at one of Connors's men.

Rikki stared at me, horrified. "Tell me you have something worked out."

I didn't respond. The man grabbed Rikki, who struggled to pull away. I took a step toward them when one of the armed guards stepped forward, shoving the barrel of his LSAT into my face.

"Stick out your arm," Marisa demanded.

"The hell I will," Rikki retorted. This time, she thrashed, pulling away from the man.

The guard who retrieved Rikki punched her in the face. Every muscle in my body tensed, but if I moved, I'd be dead.

Stunned, Rikki couldn't resist as Connors's man wrapped his arms around her, pulling her into his grasp. He dragged her toward Marisa.

"This won't hurt but for a second," the girl lied, dragging the blade of the sword up and down Rikki's bare arm as if it were caressing her.

Regaining her composure, Rikki jerked her arm back. The other American quickly moved to help, stepping past me and in front of the gunman.

Rikki's entire body contorted into a spiral. She pulled the first American toward her as she hooked her foot behind his left leg. In a single swift motion, she swept the man's leg out from under him as she used the man's weight to throw him into the nearest guard.

I lowered my shoulder, ramming the second American. The two of us plowed into the guard, whose trigger finger was twitchier than it should have been. The LSAT fired a burst of gunfire into the American as I rolled off him. My right hand caught the barrel of the automatic rifle, shoving it away from me as he fired again.

The volley of bullets ricocheted near the crowd, who went into immediate panic. Townspeople scattered as rounds peppered the road in front of them.

My elbow slammed into the guard's chin, and I rolled over him. The rifle pressed against both of our chests. When I finished the move, I jerked the butt from his hand. My finger slid into the trigger guard, and I squeezed it.

The telescoped magazine held about 150 bullets, and at a rate of 650 rounds per minute, it took about eleven seconds for the ammunition to feed through the firing chamber and out the barrel. Most of those rounds hit the third guard, but at least forty or so ended up in the first guard. He'd maintained his grip on the barrel for the first six seconds before the heat was too much. When he let go, I pulled the sights on him without letting off the trigger.

Rikki's American lay face down on the street. Whatever she'd done to him left him unconscious. I stood up, realizing both Connors and Marisa had taken off for the house.

"C'mon," I urged Rikki, who grabbed a Glock from the man she'd knocked out.

I picked up the other guard's LSAT, and we both started running for the gate. If they got the entry closed, we'd have to climb the fence. That would give them plenty of time to either get the drop on us or escape to the Hatteras down by the beach.

A gunshot echoed down the street, and I felt the bullet whiz past me. Turning, I saw the other guard running toward us from where he'd gone to rouse the townfolk. He dropped to one knee and lifted the rifle in his hands. In my mind, I envisioned how I looked through the scope of that gun.

Then a rock hit the man in the head. He tumbled to the side as two more townspeople converged on them—including the bartender who warned me earlier. They pelted him with stones.

"Chase!" Rikki shouted, having run ahead.

I left the villagers to deal with the gunman as I ran for the gate. The two men I'd killed in the street still lay sprawled there. I leaned over the man with the blade sticking out of his side. My hand yanked the bloody knife free from his body. Wiping the blood on the dead man's shirt, I slid the knife back into the sheath still attached at my waist.

"Chase!"

The whirring of gears started as the metal gates swung together. Rikki ran between the gap, and three steps behind her, I squeezed through with only inches to spare.

"Where are they?" Rikki asked.

"Either the house or the boat," I suggested. "Follow me."

The LSAT in my hand remained ready as I followed the walkway the guards escorted me down earlier. When we passed the pool, I glanced down at the Hatteras. It still floated at anchor. Not that either of them had time to weigh anchor and get away.

"The dinghy's still on the shore," Rikki pointed out.

I followed her finger as she pointed to the white inflatable pulled up on the beach.

"They brought me ashore in it," she explained. "I think it was the only way out to the boat."

My attention focused on the house. We approached the steel door. If they'd locked it, we might have trouble getting inside. It wasn't impossible, but I'd need a minute to figure it out. My hand turned the knob. When the door opened, I shook my head.

"Why didn't they lock it?" Rikki asked, wondering the same thing I did.

"My guess is these criminal masterminds were too scared."

I stepped inside, tracking the barrel between the two entry points to the room.

"You stupid bitch," Connors shouted from somewhere in the house. "You should have just killed them."

"Don't you talk to me that way!" Marisa screamed back.

I gestured for Rikki to go through the door on the other side of the room. Most of the arguing seemed to come from the closest door, but I suspected the rooms connected.

Stepping on the tile floor in the hallway, I crept down the corridor toward an open door. As I stepped closer, Connors appeared in the corridor. A frantic look turned into shock when he saw me.

I grabbed him by the front of his shirt and jerked him away from the door, slamming him into the other wall.

Behind me, I heard the click of a hammer being pulled back into firing position,

"Tell you what, Mr. Chase," Señorita Soria announced. "I'll let you shoot the bastard before I kill you."

Connors slid down the wall until he settled on the tile floor. His face twisted with a mixture of fear and resolution. There was no scenario where I could turn around fast enough to shoot her before the revolver in her hands fired.

"Go ahead," she ordered. "Or I can do it once you are dead."

The gunshot echoed through the hallway, and Señorita Soria fell against me before collapsing on the floor. Rikki stepped up beside me, aiming the Glock at Connors.

"I wonder if the keys are in the boat?" I asked out loud.

Rikki replied, "Hell if I know. Are you going to shoot him?"

My eyes locked on Connors. "Yeah," I said, firing one shot into the man's chest.

31

The autopilot on the Hatteras clicked as it adjusted its heading. I sat on the bridge watching the blue waves push over the bow. Whitecaps foamed and spread as far as I could see, and the result was a cruise that rocked the yacht in every direction. Two big diesel motors drove the hull forward though, keeping us on track, even if we'd lost some speed.

For the first few hours out of Las Higuerillas, the engines had us clipping over calm seas at about sixteen knots—a rate that could get us back to the west coast of Florida in three days. When the wind and waves picked up, I pulled the throttle back to about twelve knots. Now, we were sludging forward at eight to ten knots.

I hadn't recalculated our ETA, mostly because I didn't care. When we left Marisa Soria's beachside house, we found the Hatteras fairly well-provisioned with full fuel tanks. Since neither of us entered Mexico legally, it seemed just as wise to slip out the same way.

Besides, three to four days at sea was a well-deserved break from the last few days. And Rikki needed the rest. She offered to take a watch after we set out, but I declined, telling her to catch some sleep. I was still rolling from the few hours on the plane last night.

So far, she'd been asleep for nearly nine hours. I'd dozed lightly once we were out in the open water. Now that it was dark, I remained a bit more vigilant, watching the radar. For the moment, there was not a single soul within fifteen miles of us.

When I did a night watch, I found myself staring up at the stars. The romantic in me would say I was counting them, but it was impossible to consider numbering even ten when the galaxy spreads out above.

"Hey," Rikki said, popping her head up from below deck.

"Morning gorgeous. How are you feeling?"

"I'm starving," she replied. "Want something to eat?"

"Sure." I nodded.

A few minutes later, she reappeared with two bowls of white rice with cheese and chicken. Rikki practically leaped forward to grab a bowl, claiming she was starving. I'd found the galley while she was sleeping, so I wasn't as famished as she had been.

"Where are we?" she asked.

"Roughly 120 miles east of Mexico. I could give you the exact coordinates if you want them."

"No, I think I'm good. I need to call Sam somehow," she remarked. "He'll be worried to death."

"It looks like the cartel spared no expense," I told her. "There's internet on the boat. La Señorita Soria went all out. She's got that satellite type that's supposed to work anywhere."

"Great," Rikki said. "You don't think they can track it?"

"Probably," I admitted. "Let's use it pretty soon before anyone thinks to ping it."

Rikki nodded, slipping into the navigator's seat opposite me. "I'm still exhausted," she commented. "Does that go away?"

"Eventually," I assured her. "Not all. It never does. But knowing you, life gets more manageable."

She scooped a few bites of rice and cheese into her mouth. As she chewed, I felt her eyes on me. I set my bowl on the helm before leaning back in the chair.

"What's on your mind?" I asked.

"Connors," she answered. "Do you regret killing him?"

"Why would I?"

"He was defenseless at the time," she explained.

I nodded, taking in her thoughts.

"Rikki, let me ask you something," I said. "Why would waiting for him to have a gun make it better?"

"It would be self-defense."

"I think it was," I replied.

She furrowed her brow.

"What would happen if I'd let him live?"

Shrugging, she answered, "I don't know."

"Do you think we could have taken him with us?"

She shook her head.

"Me either," I confirmed. "However, I know that he wanted us dead. In lieu of that, he might want to harm us. You just killed the leader of the Soria Cartel. While they might only be growing, we don't know how much power she had. Or if there is a successor. If Connors survived, he'd be able to tell them not exactly who we were, but enough for someone to find us. If he wanted to take matters into his own hands, he could hunt us down himself. In that regard, the safest course of action was to eliminate him."

She stirred her rice slowly, staring into the bottom of the bowl. "I guess I understand that," she remarked. "It just seems to go against your personality."

I shrugged. "He planned to kill us both. If I hadn't shot him, he'd still want to kill us. While that's not necessarily the reaction I'd take with just anyone who hated me like that, Connors nearly succeeded."

She straightened up. "Did I tell you thank you for coming to get me?"

"Which time?" I asked.

She grinned, but her face grew solemn. "It's odd. In the woods, I never worried about what was going to happen," she explained. "But when that plane took off, I thought that was it. There was no way you'd find me."

I leaned across and cupped her cheek with my hand. "I thought the same thing."

Rikki placed her hand over mine and moved forward to kiss me. After several seconds, she pulled away.

"I need to message Sam."

I nodded, standing up. Her eyes drifted to my belt.

"Is that my knife?" she asked.

My hand pulled the blade from the scabbard. "This one?" I asked. "I think I took it off one of the cops."

"Yeah, the bastard stole it from me," she growled.

I spun the knife around in my hand, presenting her with the hilt. "Have it back," I offered.

"Sam gave it to me," she explained. "It's more than just sentimental. He got it from his mentor during his IRA days."

"No need to explain," I assured her.

Rikki took the blade. Her mouth turned up slightly as she examined it.

"Is that blood?" she asked.

I shrugged.

"Dammit, I saw you pull it out of the guy on the street," she stated. "I didn't realize."

"It seemed like a nice weapon," I remarked. "I hated to leave it where some Mexican cop would snag it."

She kissed me again, pushing her hands and the knife behind her back.

"Was that my finder's fee?" I asked.

"Oh, no," she retorted. "That's the deposit for the reward I owe you."

I waggled my eyebrows at her in the most Groucho of ways.

She let out a slight giggle, but she might have faked it. "I'm going to figure out how to email Sam," she told me. "You will want to consider washing those clothes. I'm pretty sure there's blood on them."

"Sam only got me one set," I replied.

"It's not like I packed a bag," she responded. "Guess we'll be having a couple of no-clothes days at sea."

With that, she vanished below deck. A smile spread across my face. I reached over and pulled the throttle back just a hair, dropping us to about six knots—enough to push through the waves. It would only add an extra half day to our trip, but I wasn't in a hurry.

An hour later, Rikki appeared on the steps. She'd followed her own advice and showered. Now, she stood naked in the cabin's light. I examined her slowly, reminding myself of each curve of her body.

"Your turn," she ordered. "I'll take the watch."

"There's nothing out there," I told her.

"Good. I like the idea of being alone."

The Hatteras had a much bigger head than *Carina,* where I could take a shower in a pinch as long as everything in the bathroom with me got wet too. This one had its own shower—with enough room to turn around. I stayed under the stream of water for about twenty minutes. I washed the fatigues and t-shirt off in the water, rubbing them with a bar of soap. Once I'd rinsed the soap off, I carried them to the back deck, spreading them out to dry.

"Still no sign of anyone around," Rikki said when I returned to the bridge.

"That's good."

"Think we can leave the bridge unattended for a bit?" she asked, running her fingers over my bare chest.

"It seems like that might be in order," I remarked. "After all, we have an alarm on the radar."

She took me by the hand, leading me down into the cabin.

An hour later, Rikki let out a breathy gasp as she dropped back on to the bed.

"What are you going to do when you get back?" I asked her after a minute.

"Don't know," she replied. "There is still the treasure of Gasparilla out there."

"You said there wasn't a lot of factual information out there," I pointed out.

"It makes it more challenging," she told me. "I like a challenge."

"If you don't want to dive right into that, you could take some time to island hop with me. Maybe let Sam take a vacation."

"Just me and you on your little sailboat?" she asked playfully.

"Only us and the wind."

"Do we have to wear clothes?" she asked.

"Captain's rules say you never have to wear clothes outside of port."

"The captain sounds like a stickler, too."

"Oh, yeah, he is," I joked.

Rikki pulled up on her elbows and kissed me. Within seconds, we wrapped back up in each other.

As she finally drifted to sleep, I caressed her cheeks. The woman seemed at peace. I stared at her as the boat chugged along, rocking through the whitecaps. Her eyes fluttered as she dreamed. I lifted her off my arm, depositing her on her pillow.

On deck, I checked the radar again. Still alone.

I leaned against the railing, watching the black sea under a ceiling of starlight. Rikki could hopefully find whatever solace she needed in her sleep. Right now, I found myself in my own dreams, staring out across the Gulf with the waves crashing over the bow.

A sigh slipped out of my lips.

For a list of other books by Douglas Pratt
visit the author's webpage at
http://www.douglas-pratt.com/

www.ingramcontent.com/pod-product-compliance
Lightning Source LLC
LaVergne TN
LVHW050941090125
800706LV00006B/444